BOULEVARDIERS

Boulevardiers: The Greenpoint Oil Spill

by
Joel Chaffee

Rochester,
Marietta,
Brooklyn,
NY.

Boulevardiers

Joel Chaffee

'If you fall in this water, you don't drown – you become polluted to death.'

– Howard J. Lamp'l of the Army Engineers, describing Newtown Creek, off the East River.

- Quotation of the Day, *New York Times,* May 20, 1967.

1

P ressler Dog was a very good dog. His fur was dense and erratic with swirls of black, brown, and lighter and darker shades of black and brown - a color combination known as brindle. It was true, as Derik had said earlier, that he had tumors, but of these he was joyfully ignorant.

Pressler Dog was not the sort of dog one could unleash, though he was dangerous only to himself. And bumpers, Jonah supposed, holding the leash firm in his right hand, imagining Pressler's sixty pounds of body and fur catapulted skyward, his limbs stiff and patient. Pressler Dog observed to Jonah that Adrian Block had landed hereabouts in the year 16-whatever it was. Who the hell is Adrian Block?, Jonah wondered, but said nothing.

Sometime around 1940 or 1950 - the corporation could not be pegged to a specific date, or decade - the Sanyard Oil Company let loose a torrent of petroleum from several oil tanks sitting beside Newtown Creek, the thin four-mile waterway separating Brooklyn from Queens, laying off the East River. The Creek's mouth was approximate to Manhattan's intersection of 1st Avenue & 25th Street. Immobile Oil (IO), among several descendants of Sanyard Oil, has never been certain of how much oil was released into the aquifers sitting beneath Greenpoint. (The city, fortunately, obtains its water from upstate New York, and a quick peek at the water beneath Greenpoint assured the city a second look would be superfluous.)

The corporation is swift to inform the curious that the Greenpoint Oil Spill - the seventh largest oil spill in world history, which had settled forty feet below street level - was not a one-time spill like the Immobile *Haldez*, but rather an accumulation of dozens - likely hundreds, perhaps thousands - of spills, both accidental and purposeful. Spills from a host of companies who had industrialized the neighborhood in the years following the Civil War. And do not forget, IO reminds, that the largest part of the spill was caused by a massive explosion in the city's sewer system, not from anything IO had done or not done; with care or without.

Funny, Pressler Dog commented, pawing through tall weeds, sniffing dirt, tail wagging, who ever heard of a Greenpoint Oil Spill? I know, Jonah said, not touching the chain-link fence running along the Creek's edge but nevertheless intimately close to touching it. Yeah, who ever heard of a Greenpoint?

Jonah paused, as was customary in their nightly walks, and watched a man in a canoe toss a blanket onto the surface of the creek. Jonah waved to the man, who returned the gesture.

'Miguel, how is it going?'

'Si si!' Miguel called back through cupped, rough hands. He waved a red baseball cap. 'Si, Senor Jonah, very much petrol toniiiiight!' Miguel rocked the canoe - dangerously, thought Jonah - in an episode of laughter.

Miguel gathered the blanket from the creek, squeezed its contents into the bottom of his canoe, and again spread the blanket onto the creek. Jonah and Pressler Dog continued walking, Jonah waving goodbye. Miguel sold his recovered product in glass jars to the BPP refinery two blocks north of Jonah and Puffer's apartment on Morgan Avenue. Next door to the BPP was an offal dock, the smell of which was ghastly for Jonah but riveting and sacred for Pressler Dog. Jonah wondered if he would reach Morgan before Miguel, who traversed the creek nightly seeking the most lucrative tides. Jonah, afraid of the creek, instructed Pressler to double-time it. Pressler Dog responded that the only one holding up this party couldn't have double-timed it in slow-motion. Yuck yuck, Pressler, Jonah said.

Pressler waved to the passing East River Kayak Club as they passed on their weekly paddle through the creek. They waved to Pressler, and to Miguel, continuing their course back to the East River.

The Greenpoint Oil Spill, estimated to be between seventeen million to thirty million gallons of petroleum, was first noticed by an alert Coast Guard in 1978. This is when the neighborhood stopped using local water, causing the water table to rise, pushing the floating oil up and into the creek. From the height of helicopters the Guard noted a dark plume bulging into Newtown Creek in the vicinity of Meeker Avenue. (This plume, of course, *not* the same plume as the enormous discharges of polychlorinated solvents known as the Meeker Avenue Plume, an inheritance from dry cleaners like Acme Steel, Spic and Span, and Klink Cosmo.) A two-year investigation later, the Guard handed the case to the State Department of Environmental Conservation, who perfected the prose and grammar of their report for a decade before asking Immobile Oil to please, pretty please, with no warnings and no fines and no harsh language, please clean up the mess, when you get a chance. We know you lost a few billion dollars to those irritable Alaskans, but please, the people are angry; and ill. IO responded that sure, we'll help out, we want to do our part and, by the way, we spilled another thirty-five thousand gallons into the ground a month or so ago, December of '88 or January of '89, and when we looked into it: Huh, what do you know, there's another few million gallons down here! Is that the spill you're referring to, Department of Environmental Conservation?, because we've just been scratching our heads wondering what in tarnation you've been talking about, and we'd like to come totally clean with everything starting *now*.

Environmental Commissioner, Domas D. Burlin, certainly an adorable silly billy, said, 'The industry lost seventeen million gallons of product and they didn't even miss it.' Burlin surely thought those IO fellows to be quite a crew of chuckleheads. When IO failed to mention to the state a new fifty thousand gallon heating oil spill in Staten

Island Sound in 1990, they were fined $500,000 and told not to do it again.

Once let a man, Pressler Dog quoted, snout pointed to the heavens, grow up amidst Brooklyn's cobblestones, with the odor of Newtown Creek and Gowanus Canal ever in his nostrils, and there's no place in the world for him except Brooklyn.

Jonah said that he had once seen a dead whale in Gowanus Canal.

Yuck yuck, Jeffries, Pressler Dog said, disbelieving, yuck yuck.

Now a far ways behind them, Jonah watched Miguel quickly row his canoe to shore, retrieve a fishing pole, and cast his line into the Creek. Miguel was not in such a hard place that he ate Creek fish, what there was of them. But he had spotted, down creek, Patrolman John Corcoran approaching from the east in his rowboat. Corcoran was the only marine traffic policeman on the Creek. As the War Department's numbers illustrated that the Creek had more traffic than the Mississippi River, the Patrolman's task was to keep Creek traffic moving - a daunting enterprise for any one, let alone from the position of a rowboat. Corcoran, chatting with Jonah on occasion, had claimed for three years running that the city would make good on its promise to buy him a motorboat in the next fiscal year, which inevitably became the *next* fiscal year, and so on.

The size of Immobile Oil's balls cannot be overstated. Almost twenty years after the Coast Guard had found the spill lurking about the Creek, the corporation was not yet halfway completed with the cleanup. To add sass to the open-handed slap that was the cleanup, when the corporation was finally ordered to clean the spill, they used the most dated, ancient technology available, not the new and better equipment designed and built with federal funds. When the state asked IO to please, you must use the new equipment, IO said - in a fit - Fine, you don't like the way we're cleaning it up? Then we just won't do it at all. And IO had stopped pumping the oil out from beneath Greenpoint. 'We'll be here until the job is done and done right,' Barry

Wood, IO spokesman, assured the community. This, plainly, was what everyone was afraid of.

There was a difference, the Department of Environmental Conservation said, between the Greenpoint Oil Spill and the Meeker Avenue Plumes. The Plumes *moved*, first of all, inching with the groundwater from the four major deposits of chlorinated solvents beneath the neighborhood towards Newtown Creek. Also, the Plumes were perhaps fifty feet below street level, meaning only their vapors were, at present, a danger. The Spill, floating atop the water table just twenty feet below the surface, did not, largely, move; save for when rain caused the water level to rise, which pushed the topmost oil into the Creek. The Spill and the Plumes did not intermingle, save for erratic gases here or a puddle there. Having two separate causes, they were two distinct problems.

Pressler Dog jumped, surprised, at the 'blurbp' sound of a large barge full of something heavy sinking completely beneath the surface of the water. Pressler Dog, joking only partially, claimed for a moment that he had thought it was old wooden leg Stuyvesant, coming to kick the disobedient. (Pressler Dog's head had been filled with all sorts of garbage and folklore by the pups who had grown up in the neighborhood.) Wooden leg Stuyvesant was said to haunt the grounds of the creek nearest the East River, where the federal government had stored 'green powder' in a large house. This property, abandoned by the Feds in 1850, was later sold to the French during World War I, who used the area as a military and munitions base. Jonah told Pressler Dog that the area was presently a parking lot for massive trucks and an oil tank. Pressler Dog sniffed, to indicate that he thought Jonah did not have the courage to believe in and be afraid of Governor Stuyvesant - nor did Jonah know anything about the old munitions site, so just shut the you-know-what up about it and watch me urinate on this enormous pile of garbage beneath the Kosciuszko Bridge.

'It is illustrative of us,' Pressler Dog said, eyeing some pipes nearby and quoting Riverkeeper's report, 'that the problem is not the discharging of toxic chemicals into Newtown Creek, but doing so without the appropriate Clean Water Act permits.'

Pressler Dog, having a second sight of which Jonah was totally unaware, watched the horizons of Brooklyn, Queens and Manhattan fill with dense clouds of smoke as Dutch soldiers fired from Forts Willem Hendrick, Hamilton and Battery Weed, saluting the arrival of Governor Stuyvesant to the New City in May 1647. Pressler never bothered to relate his visions to Jonah, not because Jonah would disbelieve them, but because Pressler Dog did not see anything unusual in one time period overlapping another. That is, he figured that Jonah saw the same sights, and thought them unremarkable. Far from sending out salutary volleys, Pressler squirted his last into the garbage and sneezed rapidly and repeatedly his disgust for the arriving wooden legged Governor.

It was only fair play that whatever oil IO did remove from beneath the homes and business of Greenpoint, it shipped to a refinery in New Jersey and sold. And if they happened to spit more pollutants into the Creek by way of cleaning the spill, what was that between friends? The state, meanwhile, was thinking of asking for federal assistance with the cleanup, which would mean a Superfund designation by the Environmental Protection Agency, who had already said they saw no need to test local homes and business for dangerous levels of benzene and tuleune, in vapor form, farting from the spill and traversing through cracks and crannies into residences. Besides, we didn't find anything all that exciting when we tested the neighborhood, which demonstrates that our decision not to test the neighborhood was correct. This sublime paradox, Pressler Dog thought, could only be attributed to a state. Or a Jeffries.

Yuck yuck, Pressler Dog, yuck yuck.

Pressler Dog told Jonah to go join Concerned Citizens of Greenpoint, or Greenpoint Against Smell and Pollution, or the Newtown

Creek Monitoring Committee if he were so interested in the social justice of the thing. Jonah said, Pressler Dog, you must be crazy, telling me to join groups that are sure to have been - or are sure to be - infiltrated with all sorts of spies. This is the United States, Pressler Dog, home of not only the brave but of the CIA, the FBI, the NSA, the N-.

Pressler Dog balked that yes, he knew the whole vegetable soup litany, as though any of those folks gave enough of a damn about Greenpoint to spy on anyone, let alone Jonah Jeffries. Jonah reminded Pressler Dog that it was well known that the NKVD (the Soviet Union's secret police) was all over the neighborhood looking for expatriates. And that while Greenpoint could boast Representative Shirley Chisholm, it also had to claim Representative Samuel Dickstein. Dickstein, Pressler Dog!, Jonah said, who took so many pains to create what finally became the House Committee of Un-American Activities and route out the Commies that he got himself on the payroll of the Cheka, until he lost his seat and was no longer of any use to the Kremlin.

Pressler Dog said, Did you know that Cheka means Extraordinary Commission? Ha!, Jonah said, does the CIA mean Extraordinary Rendition? No, Jonah, Pressler Dog said, it means Central Intelligence Agency. Jonah said, And those fellows are on what Jesus would call an Extraordinary Commission. Pressler Dog, eyeing a bitch being walked along Scott Avenue, said something about an extraordinary emission.

Many of the barges that sank in the Creek, and in the East and Hudson Rivers, as well as Jamaica Bay, belonged to the PHILE Foundation (PF), a construction company who did not own property on the Creek to clutter. The city was growing uncharacteristically testy with PF and its debris, particularly because of the fifty-three million dollar contract PF had recently signed with the Parks Department, to install a walkway beneath the Williamsburg Bridge.

A local group, Riverkeeper, had paid to have more rigorous (practical?) testing conducted near the areas indicated on the EPA's own map of the Meeker Avenue Plumes, to ascertain the extent of the problem. The Meeker Avenue Plumes were two lakes of pollutants sitting beneath about one-hundred homes in the easternmost corner of Greenpoint. This corner, home to Jonah, Manfred and Pressler Dog, was tucked between the Brooklyn-Queens Expressway to the south, the Creek to the north and east. The Plumes were mostly comprised of PCE and TCE - which Pressler Dog dared Jonah to try and pronounce their full names, Jonah declining. Riverkeeper's test results were as terrifying as they were predictable, and the state paid them little mind.

Finally, the EPA did test, and did report their test's findings, which illustrated - in direct opposition to the findings of community groups, whose biases are well known - that there's nothing to worry about here, but of course we can't really be certain because it would take longer than one year to complete a thorough report on the issue, and is Greenpoint really worth the effort? This EPA report was draft by four individuals - two of whom were Lockheed Smartin (LS) employees; a third was a former employee.

What's that got to do with anything, Pressler Dog?, Jonah scoffed.

Well Jonah, Pressler Dog continued, with characteristic coincidence, the EPA had, just recently, signed a contract with Lockheed Smartin worth $230 million. This government contract required LS to, among other responsibilities, respond in situations concerning the Clean Water Act, the Environmental Conservation Act, and other radical legislation. If Newtown Creek were declared a Superfund site by the US Senate (and what loony thought this possible?) LS would have no choice but to start the egregiously expensive and time-consuming cleanup. And for what? Greenpoint? Queens? *Brooklyn?*

Jonah did not ponder leaving Greenpoint as he and Pressler Dog wandered towards home, walking the frightful edge of the Creek. Across the water in Queens the Sitibank building rose into the ether

like a castle, its moat a lobby with ID-scanning turnstiles. He did wonder exactly what kind of lung disease would eventually cease his respi-
ratory system. But no guesses tonight. He watched electric light play
upon the water, giving the illusion that the Creek was flowing towards the East River, though the Creek did not flow. The water's
surface glimmered in ebbing circles and avenues of oil, kerosene, mercury and naphtha. Orange and dark, mythic, flammable. The sludge
in the Creek was so pervasive that there was no oxygen in the water.
When a large tide from the East River swelled the Creek with
fresh(er) water and the miracle of fish, the fish either swam out with
the tide or died in the Creek, making for easily caught dinners for Jose
Jose and family, Jonah thought.

The hum of the enormous ovals at the Newtown Creek Sewage
Treatment Plant turned to a whine as Pressler Dog and Jonah circum-
vented Whale Creek, a tributary of Newtown. The Plant was lit at
night in a strange and alien purple flame, like God's own fire, which
Jonah never stared at too long, for fear. At the familiar sound, Jonah
imagined the ovals churning cookie batter, instead of seventy-five
percent of the city's sewage. Over 6,000 tons of which was carried to
Sandy Hook Bay (it's only New Jersey) and discharged through open-
ings in the bottom of the sewage-carrying vessel.

He tossed handful of grass onto the water's surface and imagined it
floating into New York Harbor and the Atlantic beyond. Oil from the
spill sometimes, on a whim, jumped or spurted or leapt into the treatment plant, and the whole sludge-making process would be halted,
the oil destroying the bacteria (aroused by oxygen) which broke the
sewage down into sludge - a preferential form of the stuff. Pressler
Dog, watching the floating grass with Jonah, sang a little ditty about
hayseeds going back to the country.

In 1891, the self-appointed Brooklyn Smelling Committee had
voted Long Island City, across the water from Greenpoint, one of the
city's 'smelliest places.' (Pressler Dog said, Big deal, I got one of the
city's smelliest places right here.) Six years later, the *Fort Worth Reg-*

ister hyperbolically reported that merely a trolley ride over the Creek left one cleaning 'odiferous remnants of its atmosphere' from their person for several weeks. The neighborhood knew enough about the Creek that windows were shut when the spill farted - when precipitation flooded the aquifer, which pushed the oil floating atop it into the Creek. Rainwater was also prone to flood the sewage system's tanks, which then overflowed into the Creek.

Pressler Dog trotted, sniffing and singing a song he had written and rewrote with each sightseeing trip to the Creek. It went something like,

Cadmium, PCB, naphtha and sludge,
Chromium, copper and xylene and stuuuuuuff.
Oh, Newtown Creek, I am one of your own,
One whiff of your pleasures and I'm stoned to the bone.
Arsenic and benzene: you've got it right here,
But wooden leg Stuyvesant 's the feariest fear!

It is true, as Immobile Oil is persistent in stating, that much of the spill beneath Greenpoint - and much of Greenpoint's horrendous environmental condition - are contributions from a litany of sources. Several dry-cleaning facilities spent a half-century dumping chlorinated solvents into the ground, as well as toxins into the Creek, including TCE (trichloroethylene) and PCE (tetrachloroethylene). The Diamond Rendering Co. tossed fats and whatever else into the Creek and were charged by the city with 'polluting the air with malodorous emissions.' Electricity provider Keypan (formerly Brooklyn Union Gas Company) spewed coal tar into the Creek and buried it into the dirt - unless it was recycled in the form of road for the streets of Greenpoint. Emissions from the Non-Ferrous Processing Corporation prompted the testing of hundreds of local school children for harmful levels of lead oxide in the blood. (The Council of the Environment of New York City found that the highest concentrations of airborne lead in all of Gotham's glory could be found, where else?, in Williamsburg and Greenpoint.) And, though he could not say how it affected public health more than one-hundred years later, Jonah forsook meat (for at least a moment) at the sight of a former horse-slaughterhouse, whose meat was reportedly 'corned and put up for export as family beef.' Thank God they only sold it to the UK!, he thought, and not domestically. Also to be included in the accumulated evil of the whole were Greenpoint's limitless factories, responsible for fertilizer, glue, smelting, fat-rendering, animal corpse-processing, sawmilling, paint works, sugar refineries, automotive recycling, and natural gas.

Jonah breathed deeply, the warm evening sting of Creek air burning his lungs like a cigarette, but without the guilt associated with smoking. He wanted to taste a Newtown Pippin apple, once a favorite of Thomas Jefferson and many in the New World. But the strain of apple made famous in Green Point in the 17th and 18th centuries had died out, and Pippins were now grown almost exclusively in the Northwest US.

Across the water in Queens the former Felps Bodge (FB) copper refinery site housed large, ominous trucks. After the sale of the property in 1983 to the US Postal Service, the land - choked with PCBs, heavy metals, et al. - was returned to Felps Bodge by the Feds, with an interest fee and cleaning bill to boot. Bodge - now owned by Breeport McSmoran - had been able to lease all but the fifteen feet of land closest to the Creek, where they remained responsible for keeping the soil and groundwater from worsening the condition of the Creek. Jonah made a comment about Breeport McSmoran relieving the Democratic Republic of Congo of its coltan, copper and gold. Pressler Dog, chuckling, returned that wooden leg Stuyvesant had tried to get there first.

Were the Felps Bodge site cleaned, it was to become a terminal in a new track for freight trains between Long Island, Queens, Brooklyn, Staten Island and New Jersey. Known as the Cross-Harbor Rail

Tunnel Project - plans for which went back to the 1890s - the FB area was so disastrously contaminated that the cost of cleanup halted any advance made on the Tunnel Project.

It was said that a lovely marsh in the old salt flats of Greenpoint, jutting from the site of present day Freeman Street into the East River, had given the neighborhood its name. Sailors, spying the salt marshes and swamps (now entirely obliterated) knew themselves arrived to the new city in what was the busiest Creek in the New World. Pressler Dog thought this legend hogwash, since the place used to be called Cherry-Point, and what was the Cherry for, Jonah?, the high incidence of Redmen? To which a prude Jonah scolded Pressler Dog for his caustic and offensive language, Pressler Dog responding that he had a caustic and offensive something right here. . . .

An enormous snapping turtle emerged from the Creek and waddled up the black beach. Were it Lazarus or Tadeusz Kosciuszko it would not have been more shocking to Pressler and Jonah. Manfred often claimed to see them from his tiny VW on the Kosciuszko Bridge, the turtles not darting through traffic but being overtaken by it. State tests had found that dried Creek sediment was one-tenth oil. How then could *Chelydra serpentina serpentina* - who lived almost exclusively underwater - survive down there?

Pressler Dog wondered aloud to Jonah if Jonah had told his father, Mr. Congregationalist Reverend Jeffries, that there were no Congregationalists in Greenpoint. Catholics, Methodists, Russian Orthodox, Dutch Reformed, Episcopalians, Baptists, Universalists - wasn't there even a mosque around here? Jonah had, indeed, Pressler Dog, rubbed it in with the old man. Of course, Jonah admitted, the old man had rubbed back, saying that the Congregationalists were content to leave the Creek and its three billion gallons of polluted stormwater and sewage to their somewhat mentally blocked but nevertheless upstanding brethren in the less . . . . *refined* denominations.

The list of the Creek's former oil refineries - BCF, C.H. Nichol's, Gulf, King's County Oil Works, Platt's, Queen's County, Stone &

Fleming, Bayside Oil, Morgan Oil, Paragon, Amoco - is deceptive, since they all originated from the patriarch, Mockefeller/Sanyard Oil. And eventually - through Immobile Oil, BPP, and Shevron - were re-united. The periodical history of the area is one of pollution, explosions, fires. An 1895 eruption at the King's County Oil Works sent seven tanks of oil into the Creek. An explosion in 1919 did worse. It is almost misleading to point out specific instances of massive pollution of the Creek and environs. It would be more accurate to site specific instances when the Creek and environs were *not* being polluted. But here the record runs dry.

In addition to the previous litany of pollution sources, Greenpoint could also boast dozens of waste transfer stations (old and new), easily hundreds of EPA 'Toxic Release Inventory' and 'Right To Know' facilities, construction companies (largely disposing of waste via barges in the Creek, or just the streets of Greenpoint itself), and over one hundred pipes pumping the city didn't care what incessantly into the Creek, daily.

Aside from industrial pollution, an 1873 *New York Times* article identified another problem: That the Creek was 'overrun with corpses to a remarkable extent.' Perhaps the preponderance of industry and poverty in the slums along the Creek, and access to the Penny, Vernon Avenue and Greenpoint Avenue Bridges, were all a poor bastid could hope for. 'Why people go and drown themselves in this muddle and unpleasant stream,' the *Times* chuckled, 'when they have all New-York Harbor before them where to choose, is entirely unaccountable.' No doubt transportation systems have improved since the late 19th century, and contemporary Greenpointers will have recourse to the resplendent Harbor the *Times* proffered.

Pressler Dog commented that, when the time came, Newtown Creek would do just fine by him and, he hoped, by Jonah and Manfred as well.

In the old days, the Dutch Northeast India Company made payment for what became Brooklyn and Queens to the Canarsee tribe with 'Eight Fathoms of Duffel, Eight Fathoms of Wampum, Twelve Kettles, Eight Adz and Eight Axes, with some Knives, Beads and Awls.' And not a little military persuasion!, Pressler Dog guffawed. By 1638, a Scandinavian - Dirck 'the Norman' Volckersten - owned the peninsula then known as Green Point. Happily for him, Dirck was a shipbuilder, a trade that flourished on the shores of the Creek. In the 19th century, the renowned Union ship the *Monitor* was made and launched in Green Point, before fighting the Confederate *Virginia* (originally the Union's, who called it the *Merrimack*) and being quickly decommissioned. As one local historian jabs, 'None of Greenpoint's ships were particularly seaworthy.' Nevertheless, the industry swelled, producing the *Grand Republic*, the most famous ship of its day; the *Telenade*, a transport for slaves from Africa to New Orleans before she joined the oil business; and the *Everglade*, later renamed the *Savannah* while employed defending Confederate coast from Union attack.

Pressler Dog and Jonah hedged Kingsland Avenue down to Norman, the heavy air of the BPP site instantly making Jonah's eyes red. Kinglarmo, a friend of Miguel's, passed Pressler and Jonah on Norman Avenue. Kinglarmo was hauling slaughter-house waste and other manure from Messrs. Savage & Co. on Maspeth Creek (one of Newtown's tributaries) to the old French depot on the East River. The wagon of waste was drawn by an old, green Ford Explorer. The wagon, Jonah said, was so rancid it would, in the words of his great-grandmother, knock a maggot off of a gut-cart. Pressler Dog asked what the hell a gut-cart was. Jonah replied that while he did not know how a traditional gut-cart appeared, Kinglarmo's Ford Explorer - pine green and beat to hell - fit the bill as well as anything he'd been privileged enough to see.

Kinglarmo had, he'd told them, purchased the SUV from a rich woman upstate. Each side of the Explorer had been stenciled with the legend 'The Horning.' Kinglarmo had never explained his company's name to Jonah, who had not asked. Pressler Dog, familiar with both

Kinglarmo and the French depot, knew all about The Horning, but said nothing, not wanting to get into a whole thing explaining the US Senate Select Committee on Intelligence to Jonah, who was sometimes slow on the take.

In 1660 Dutch Governor Stuyvesant was delivered a 'petition' which stated, 'Fourteen Frenchman and Dutchman Pieter Janse Wit, their interpreter, have arrived here.' Janse Wit - no doubt as beloved by the Dutch as Benedict Arnold by the Union - settled in what is now Greenpoint, a gift from the departing Governor, who called it the Township of Bushwick. Janse Wit had four daughters, who married well: a Meserole, a Van Zandt, a Provoost and a Bennett. For the next couple centuries, these four families populated and cultivated the isolated spurt on Brooklyn's hump, Green Point. Separated from Queens and Manhattan by water, and from the rest of the burgeoning city of Brooklyn by lack of roadway, the families employed slave labor (King's County being the largest slaveholding county north of the Mason-Dixon) to grow and then ship produce to Manhattan by way of water. It is hoped, in contemporary Greenpoint, that this water access to Manhattan will one day be regained.

Pressler Dog, panting heavily, said that he was lucky that Jonah was white, because if it were just a Pressler Dog walking down this abandoned warehouse block, all black and brown as I am, the NYPD car which just passed would have stopped and frisked me. And I'm holding, Jonah, said Pressler Dog. I'm holding big time.

In that case, Jonah said, we should start heading for home, as I want some of what you're holding, and I must be meeting with Tater come morning. Oh, is Tater back from behind the Iron Curtain?, Pressler Dog asked, and if so what did he bring me?

In 1834 Neziah Bliss arranged northern Brooklyn into a navigable series of streets with room for homes. Industry, thought Jonah with affection, exploded. Oil, lumber-yards, docks, chemical manufacturers, distilleries and mills bought property on the Creek. In 1835 Brooklyn, officially, enveloped all of Williamsburg and Bushwick, including Green Point. By 1870, the nation's first oil refineries, kerosene refinery, and a population of Dutch, French, English, Scotch, Irish and Scandinavian had arrived in the neighborhood and were performing the intense labor of shipbuilding, of moving lumber, and learning to use the new industrial machinery. Former slaves abounded. Before the turn of the century, Greenpoint's northern tip was home to more immigrants than natives. Later, troubled times and martial law in Eastern Europe and Asia brought the Russian and Pole. The outermost rim of Greenpoint, along Newtown Creek, is a Polish city featuring assorted tourists from the sticks, like Jonah and Manfred, who were predominantly employed in Manhattan. It was obvious to Greenpoint's Poles - thirty percent of the population - that these interlopers were not looking for more than a crashing pad before they were making enough money to be delivered unto residences in Manhattan.

Pressler Dog suddenly thrust his snout out and up in an orgy of sniffing. When Jonah's head ached in a familiar, radiative way, he realized that they were just outside Nashional Gryd's Greenpoint Energy Center, ten acres inaccessible to the public and a declared State Superfund Site. Energy centers were greatly intimidating to the 20th century man from the sticks who still greatly revered the power of electricity. Nashional Gryd, an international conglomerate, had purchased Keypan years before. Part of the company's Greenpoint site was a waste transfer station. Even if it's only construction waste, Pressler Dog sniffed, it's still *waste*, beautiful odiferous *waste* and just *let me at it*. Jonah held the leash firm and pulled Pressler Dog from the hole he had begun digging beneath Keypan's fence. Jonah wondered aloud if things wouldn't be better on the Creek if the Feds commandeered the industrial agora, as they had during WWII to manufacture aluminum for the P-47 Thunderbolt, the P-38 Lightning and other fighter planes that cavorted above Germans and Japanese. Aluminum, being light, allowed for faster planes and extra fuel tanks, which were themselves disposable. This period of aluminum manufacturing accounted for much of the molybdenum in the Creek; but at least the Feds had been honest about what they were tossing into the water. Pressler Dog quipped that Molybdenum was his favorite heavy metal band. Jonah repeated the old joke, She wanted to know me coming and going, so I gave her a Newtown Creek. Pressler Dog laughed, responding, I got that shit all *over* her toilette.

2

Mr. Manfred Puffer arrived to the gathering just twenty minutes before his lifelong friend, Mr. Jonah Jeffries, who was forty minutes late. Manfred, tall and large with a massive clean-shaven face beneath a mass of messy dark hair, wiped cigarette ash from his hand onto his sky blue pants as he entered the apartment building. Minutes later, annoyed with the guilt of tardiness, Jonah stood outside of the building, delaying his entrance, reading a newspaper and finishing a bland deli coffee. He glanced at the brick building to be sure it was there before resting his elbow against it. Jonah had difficulty imagining a world in which 'late' had anything to do with 'party,' but his sister, Mrs. Tabitha Jeffries, had instructed him to be punctual: 8:00pm. 'Early if you can manage,' she'd said days earlier on the phone. 'Like 7:30? 7:15? I've gotta pick up Mom from Hospice beforehand-'

'Why is Mom coming? Is this party so imperative?'

'7:30. 7:15 if you can. I gotta-' and she had hung up the phone.

Mrs. Jeffries was dependent upon Hospice care yet again. The Jeffries family had, with incredulity but gratefulness, declined the unique, never before offered 'frequent customer discount' extended by softhearted Hospice representatives. It was her melanoma, again, which had something to do with Syracuse, New York's own Onondaga Lake and environs, but there is no time for that here.

Both Manfred and Jonah were developing sublime and dystopian illnesses that had not only to do with their Greenpoint - the Garden Spot of America, as former Congressman John Rooney described it - neighborhood in Brooklyn, but with air, earth and even fire. Specifically, Jonah's stomach cancer had to do with the neighborhood's intolerably tolerated levels of radon, the largest pool of which (Radium) sat beneath Jonah's most beloved bakery, the Polska Bread Factory. While Manfred's leukemia had to do with the neighborhood's unacceptably accepted levels of benzene, emanating from the plumes near the McDonald's on Meeker Avenue; and the multi-hued puddles - 'the moat,' he termed them - Manfred's 1991 VW Gulf splashed through to obtain entrance to the White Castle on Grand Street. Though, to be fair, anyone could ask, 'Hey, wasn't Manfred's cancer of the auditory system caused by cadmium and Jonah's limb amputation by dieldrin?,' and it would have been, if not truthful, plausible.

It went without saying that both of them had asthma.

Greenpoint, and neighboring Williamsburg, boasted an impressive collection (indeed, dozens) of waste stations and facilities - waste not only 'hazardous' and 'extremely hazardous' but also radioactive - as well as a couple dozen petroleum and natural gas tanks. Almost one-hundred oil tanks sat upon Mother Earth's crust on the banks of the ethereal and quaking Newtown Creek, which ran between northern Brooklyn and southern Queens. It all reminded Jonah of the Jewish response to the kindly comment, 'You look well.' 'What, there is something should be wrong with me?'

That neither Manfred nor Jonah had visited a physician in nearly a decade was excusable only in that some of us cannot (or will not?) navigate the indifferent and expensive web known to us as the health care system - which at least has to do with 'system' if not 'health' or 'care.' But this litany of illnesses was, perhaps blessedly, a secret from the boys, who were more concerned with the practical matters of the present day.

Inside the apartment building, on the second of four floors, Mr. Derik Merrill picked, with a tussle, a sliver of roast beef from between two molars with a mint-flavored toothpick, demonstrating little heed for where the morsel was jettisoned. He then, stolidly, belched.

'Awp. And Jes-us wept.' He held his belly and gesticulated excessively with his free hand to indicate that Ms. Victoria Knell was speaking too much. 'And Jesus wept.' He leant back against the counter, pushing his arches and toes to the wood floor in the large kitchen, eyeing the beverages on the snack table across the room. Soda, juice, water. Mrs. Leora Merrill inquired whether her rarely sated husband would like a Hi-C juice box, and did not wait for his response before taking action; nor was a response provided, save the vigorous drawing of Derik's lips on the straw, toothpick tucked behind an ear. Leora delighted herself in the moment, brown hair reflecting overhead electric light, eyes like mirrors shining a beautified version of her husband and admirer back to him.

Leora pressed a tissue into the moist hand of the weeping Victoria, who, between sniffles, spoke up to say she did not understand why she hadn't been given the entire fucking box already, goddamnit. Previously, between sniffles, she had related - in anguish - Manfred's strange request. It had been the third instance of the telling at the party alone; once more would give the day a dozen. Her long dark hair had been wrapped about her face like a niqab. Her vanilla skin gave rise in Derik's imagination to thoughts of whipped-cream and strawberry shortcake.

'Baby,' Leora said, nesting herself into Derik's body, pulling his arm about her, his thumb hooking into a belt-loop of her blue jeans, 'any story that ends-'

'Don't say it.' Victoria had momentarily quieted. 'I don't want to hear it again.'

The apartment, for its size, had few rooms. An elegant but perhaps glorified foyer upon entrance: attached to the doorframe was a dark wicker awning, itself decorated with various species of synthetic vines and flowers. An antique streetlamp hung on the underside of the awning. Beyond the foyer a large living room. A kitchen. Beyond that a bathroom, a bedroom. The apartment's owners, Mr. and Mrs. Timothy and Cassie Dennison, family friends, had agreed to host the evening's event with the stipulation that they not be invited.

Manfred was immediately conversing with the youngest of the Jeffries, Mrs. Joelle Ptooly, whose fiancé. Mr. Xavier Ptooly, was expected shortly. Manfred was quite ready for the evening to be over so that he might have a drink. He was, all in all, he told Joelle, taking it easy as the weather improved. Victoria and Manfred, though dating, had arrived separately and spent much of the evening avoiding each other and flirting with others, as was their way. They would, customarily, make amends come morning.

Jonah stamped his sneakers on the small carpet beneath the wicker awning, right hand rearranging his dark thinning hair into irregular tufts and bursts. Only a few years left with you, he thought, imagining the hair he had just lost settling onto the floor about him. His stomach ached with the burbling heat of anxiety, as he had not been able to explain to himself what kind of an event his friends, parents and even coworkers would attend at a private residence that everyone was to be on time for. The enthusiastic greeting his entrance received brought the night's first brilliant burst of panic at the thought that the party might be intended for him; and, more ominously, perhaps for his well-being. This quickly passed when nothing unusual followed the greetings. From the kitchen he heard what sounded like his lifetime friend, Derik, saying something about having copped a better feel off of a crossing guard.

'And all's I want,' Victoria said, holding back with some heroics the enormous surging sphere of tears in her throat, 'is to go back to a time before *he* requested that *I*-'

'And Jesus wept, sister. I'll say it again because you just can't hear me: And Jesus wept.' Derik swallowed the last of the juice box in one large inhalation.

'Baby.' Leora caressed his thigh through a hole in his blue jeans.

'Awp. I'm full of juice. Let's go, baby.'

Leora laughed like a gurgle of water from a small fountain. Many people fake it, but perhaps Derik and Leora were genuinely, naturally silly.

Though the congregants were many, they were familiar enough to each other that greetings were misleadingly brief. Mrs. Jeffries hugged Jonah but she was a mother and this we forgive them. From the snack table, Mr. Jeffries waved with a cup of punch, as his other hand held a precariously piled plate of finger foods. None of his children had ever seen him, in the flesh, without the beard that had now become gray as well as black. Nor did they remember (though old photographs could evidence that it was so) him with anything more atop his head than the horseshoe curve of hair that Mother trimmed fortnightly.

Tonight Tabitha, second child to Mother and Father Jeffries, was not even fleetingly amused by Jonah's tardiness. 'Did you return to Standard Time today, Jonah? Because the rest of us must have forgotten.' He smiled, said nothing. She pursed her lips and tossed her black hair as she entered the kitchen. Jonah nodded to her husband, Mr. Bryant Cross, who nodded in return, smirking beneath an overgrowth of dark beard, before following his wife into the kitchen with the soon to be extinguished hope for coffee.

'Jonah, you've heard this nonsense, right?' Derik asked without greeting. Jonah raised his eyebrows to indicate that he did not know what Derik referred to. 'This idea of Manfred's-'

'Oh, Victoria? The Newtown Creek? Sure. Heard this morning. Just after it happened. And late afternoon while at the dog dungeon.' This a reference to Jonah's place of employment, the New York Canine Hedonistic Retreat, a glorified dog kennel. 'Got an email early evening, as well.'

'And a text message.' Victoria was not to be outdone in making herself ridiculous.

'Should I expect a letter by post?'

'And a telegraph.'

'You coulda told me by carrier pigeon or black magic for all the shits I've got to give. Awp.'

Victoria, again, informed everyone that if Manfred's request for a sex act he called a Newtown Creek was not pretty to think about, it was even less pretty to participate in.

The bathroom door, just off the kitchen, suddenly opened. No one presently in the kitchen had been there when whoever was opening the bathroom door had closed it. A collective and perceivable shudder, an almost silent gasp, was emitted when Mr. Karl Whitesauce emerged, wiping his hands on his blue jeans (worn white), the *Times* crossword under his arm.

Jonah, now aware that Karl had been invited to the gathering, was momentarily convinced of his suspicion that the party was an intervention on behalf of Manfred's beleaguered liver. Why else would Karl drag himself all the way to White Plains for a party with no alcohol, and no women he could hope to leave with? Why the Dennison's in White Plains?, Jonah wondered, and hummed an old melody about hayseeds returning to the country.

'Hey, Karl, great to see you, long time, etcetera.' Jonah's verbosity surprised even himself at times, particularly when around people to whom he had nothing to say. Or rather, he thought, had plenty to say but . . . . When half of my income, he thought, is made from trademarking and commodifying the phrase 'Karl Eats It' (this after a wide and laborious graffiti campaign) asking Karl 'How is the lady?' or 'How is the job?' seemed palpably insufficient and insincere.

In response to Jonah's questions, 'How is the lady?' and 'How is the job?' Karl said that both were 'Totally totally,' while nodding his head in rapid consent.

Jonah heard Leora and Derik placing bets on why Karl had accepted what was, surely obviously, a polite invitation to an event no one present wanted him attending. Leora thought it was for use of the facilities, more of a happenstance decision to come based on location. Derik refuted this, wondering aloud what business could bring Karl from Brooklyn to White Plains; suggesting instead that Karl just may be the loneliest bastid in New York.

Jonah laughed. He was still young enough to have friends who could break his heart. What an unfortunate lot of children we are, he thought, coughing mildly.

Without announcement or invitation everyone settled into pockets of talk in the living room, fourteen individuals in all. Manfred continued to sell it to Joelle, though her and Xabier's wedding invitations had gone out only two weeks previously. 'Didn't you get yours?' she teased him.

'My inbox is backed up. How's yours?' He was endlessly amusing; likewise shameless.

A thick anxiety steadily cloaked Jonah's vision and hearing as minutes passed. He assumed the physical sensations blinding and deafening him were the articulate and voluminous release of adrenaline, the cause unknown but, somehow, narrowing its focus. Derik spoke at length and without relent - and rather engagingly. A tactless (and riotous) monologue on the personal responsibilities of Iraqi and Afghani peasants was interrupted when Tabitha clanged a spoon about the inside of a drinking glass while Bryant set a chair in the middle of the room for her to stand upon. It was not for meekness that she was instrumental in the ferocious community group United For Bitch and Justice. After ascending the chair, she turned in a circle as she talked, addressing everyone present.

'I want to thank you all for coming on such short notice.' She cleared her throat. Public speaking made her sound shy and uncertain in a false and deceptive way. 'I know Mom and Dad, you guys drove all the from-'

'Five hours!' Mr. Jeffries hollered, expensive bits of wheat crackers and asparagus dip flying from his mouth. Mrs. Jeffries reminded everyone that GK, the absent eldest, passed along his best wishes. GK was, at present, a busy bee completing paperwork. Having joined the National Guard at peacetime, it had taken a letter from Mr. Jeffries, a Reverend, to keep GK in peacetime, no matter where the Guard went. Oh, the power of the sacred letter!, Jonah had thought. The power of the holy word! Jonah, in the days preceding GK's enlistment, had in vain attempted to convince GK that peacetime, in a practical sense, did not exist for the empire. A hypothesis GK thought dubious, insubstantial and irrelevant. Not to mention rude.

It would not be hyperbole to say that Jonah Jeffries was the first of his lineage to get high on marijuana.

'Yes, so thanks, guys. I'd also like to thank Manfred-' Tabitha paused, waiting like a schoolmarm for Manfred's attention, which was not granted her until Joelle stood and walked to the bathroom, which was still redolent with what Karl had accomplished.

'Manfred, I wanted to thank you for helping me organize this thing and carpool everyone here.'

'He helped organize his own intervention?' Jonah was incredulous. 'Come on, Tabby, you don't ask the interventionee to carpool the interventionists to the intervention.' He turned to Manfred, smiling. 'Ya dumb shit. Why'd you even show?' Manfred smiled and looked away, turning to Joelle, who was not chancing the recovering restroom.

'Jonah,' Tabitha said, 'this intervention-'

'That's like walking the plank *and* being the guy who puts the plank in place.'

'Jonah, this-'

'I mean, would you voluntarily attend your own hanging, Puffer?'

'Don't call me Puffer, hayseed.'

'Jonah-'

'Puffer, you even got *Karl* to show? Well done. Kid wouldn't bother to wipe if he could get away with it.'

'Don't call me-'

'And Je-sus wept.'

'Jonah!' Tabitha was irate. 'I'm standing on a chair, damn it! *I have the floor.*'

The room silenced. Jonah and Manfred and Bryant hid laughter behind sips of water. Mr. Jeffries did not bother hiding his, cookie crumbs spraying out before him in a chortle. 'Jonah, this intervention is for *you*. It is about *you*. For *your* well-being.'

'And your reclamation!' Leora added.

'Me? An intervention for *me*?' He turned around. 'Puffer's the alcoholic. He's the one we've been talking about having an intervention for since junior prom.'

'Jonah, this is not about Manfred-'

Manfred was stern in stating that nobody needed any refresher on prom night and he'd thank Jonah to mind his own or someone might bring up someone else's pants-less you-know-what.

'And *who*' - Jonah drew the word out like an ambitious singer to express the outlandish quality of the situation - '*ooooooo. . . .*' He paused to regain his breath. '*Who* invited *Karl* to *my* intervention? Everyone knows Karl Eats It. How then could I have a useful, positive, beneficial intervention with *Karl* present? It's impostrous!, to quote Laurel. Or Hardy. The skinny one.'

'Laurel,' Manfred croaked.

Karl, uncharacteristically taking a hint, located his coat and vacated the apartment, Jonah affectionately patting his shoulder as he passed, saying, 'Karl, good to see you, buddy, you look great.' Karl responding, 'Totally totally.'

'No, no, this is obviously for Manfred. Manfred.'

'Jonah, *I* organized this.' Tabitha breathed deeply and evenly. '*I* planned it. It is for *you*.'

'I think you're wrong.'

'And Jesus wept, Jonah.' It was clear Derik had television programs that evening which he did not want to miss. 'It's for fucking you. So shut the fuck up. You're addicted to fuckin . . . . What was it, baby?'

Leora laughed like birds wouldn't twitter. 'Greenpoint, baby.'

'Right, Greenpoint. Awp. So you're fuckin . . . . addicted to the neighborhood and everyone knows it's poison, so do like everyone in Greenpoint does and move out before you're entirely polluted.' He looked to Leora. 'How was that, baby?' Her criticisms were sparse and complimentary.

'Jonah,' Tabitha said, '*Frederick* had a tumor from Greenpoint. *Andy* had a tumor from Greenpoint.' She gesticulated wildly with her hands, briefly losing her balance on the chair. 'You live *one block* from ten BPP oil tanks!'

'Sure,' Jonah replied, 'if you limit your list of the helplessly ill to all of my former roommates the case is damning, but how just?'

'Mom *has* a tumor from something, and I wouldn't be surprised if it was from Greenpoint.'

'But Mom has never spent more than a night in Greenpoint.'

'Jesus on crutches, Jonah. The goddamned *dog* has a Greenpoint tumor and that's no joke.'

Jonah admitted that it was not. He was, additionally, about to acquiesce to the prohibition on Greenpoint - if not in deed then at least, in a timely fashion, in word - but could not, finally, voluntarily subject his actions to the scrutiny of others.

But Derik needed no such submission. 'Okay, good. Tabitha, that good for you?' Tabitha, given for the briefest of miraculous moments the floor, was speechless. 'Good then. And while we're at it, what about Manfred? Let's get that over with too, since everyone here knows we're gonna do it sooner or later.'

Tabitha found her tongue. 'Ah, no, Derik, this intervention is for Jonah, not Manfred.'

'Besides,' Manfred was thorough, 'my intervention 's gotta be with all of *my* put out best friends and family and loved ones. My mom isn't even here. And I've got asthma anyway so I beat Greenpoint to the punch!'

'Christ in my pocket. Somethin' smells bad and it ain't the dog, Puffer. You're a lousy pair of lungs. Most everyone here knows you, and a couple of these dopes even *like* you a little, so don't take it for granted.'

'My intervention has got to be way more dramatic. I must throw chairs and scream hurtful things.' His large face smiled. Victoria merrily joked that Puffer's autobiography would be entitled, *Drunk, And How To Get There.* Manfred responded that the working title was merely *Flush*, but if the evening would hurry along he might oblige her. He then noted to no one specific that the room was far too warm to fart in discreetly. Victoria wondered aloud how this was relevant to him, and Manfred was quick to thank her for the reminder.

'And Jesus cried great big gobby f'ing tears, Manfred. Fine.' Derik stood on the couch and announced, 'Okay. Anyone here who gives a damn for Manfred, be here next Saturday. But Leora and me already said our piece so we're not coming.'

'Jonah.' Tabitha was composed. 'Greenpoint residents are twenty-five percent more likely to develop asthma, chronic bronchitis and emphysema than all other city residents.'

'And you don't even have to smoke!' Jonah was jovial.

'The entire neighborhood has been an industrial and public dumping ground for over two centuries. *Immobile Oil started there.*' This was damning. 'There's enough pollution beneath, in, on and around Greenpoint to pass along to the next dozen generations.'

'What a legacy!'

'It's almost a Reich,' noted Manfred.

'Stomach cancer, leukemia, autoimmune disease, brain tumors, cancers of the nervous system.' Tabitha was laying it on thick. 'Infertility-'

'Goodbye condoms!'

'Birth defects.'

'*Along* with the infertility? Sounds suspicious.'

'Myelofibrosis-'

'Does anyone here even know what that is?'

'Rare bone sarcoma!'

'Thank you, Leora,' Tabitha nodded approvingly. 'Pancreatic cancer, nervous system disorders.'

'You're just naming all of the ways God loves his children.' The tone of Jonah's joke illustrated to Tabitha that she was, inchingly, getting to him.

'The EPA determined that the contaminants of concern in the locally caught fish in Newtown Creek included cadmium, mercury, chordane-'

'Now you're just quoting from the report directly.'

'-DDT, dioxins, polychlorinated biphenyls, arsenic, lead-'

'Greenpoint is the Garden Spot of America! *And* the hometown of Mae West.'

Tabitha stopped, tired. It was enough for one evening. Jonah did not break quickly, she knew.

After the Merrill's departure, the assembled spent the remainder of the evening playing games and waiting for the appropriate moment to exit. Tabitha sat in the corner, knitting, imagining the telephone call she would one day receive concerning the news of her brother's inoperable tumor(s). Mr. Jeffries won a suspiciously quick game of *Clue* while Xabier dominated anything related to trivia (particularly with the attentive and knowledgeable GK absent), Manfred laughingly attempting to get a game of *Twister* or *Duck Duck Goose* going with Joelle. 'Et al,' he coaxed. Joelle rolled her eyes, knowing him to be something of a ham.

Jonah, indomitable when it came time for *Similes*, dismissed most of the evening thinking of his most recent ex-girlfriend, Senorita Marcenda Remedios Alvarez Johnson; and exactly how many fish from Newtown Creek it had taken to get the best of her uncle, Senor Jose Jose Morales Alvarez, a fisherman by skill and marijuana dealer by necessity (yet still also skilled), who - along with Marcenda herself, plus Jose Jose's three children - were all very much alive with diarrhea in the family's home, on some block in Greenpoint even Manfred and his car avoided without saying why. And he thought exactly of how he would pinch and tease her, and she him, eventually. Jonah had not yet responded to Marcenda's voicemail message from two days previous, not because he did not want to, but because he moved slow - and slower for ex-lovers - and in so doing recognized the meaninglessness of most human entanglements and, to compensate for this unfairness, kept an impenetrable distance - ever so difficult with a Senorita!

3

I was watching impassively. I made many of my best efforts in this way. I stood in the dark foyer of my employer, the New York Canine Hedonistic Retreat; just inside the two glass doors off 25th street. Both doors took great effort to open, particularly if one were trying to look casual about it. For reasons I never inquired about, only the right door opened; the left was always locked. Beyond the two 25th street doors stood two more glass doors, creating a small foyer, enclosed on all sides. I leaned against the wall and hoped I could not be seen by whoever was on shift inside.

I listened to the propulsive and robust noise of the large fan mounted into the wall, which blew air fresh from the foyer into the store proper. The fan leaving a soft sprinkling of dirt and dust and hair on the dog coats and other merchandise. Standing in the foyer, doors closed, the sound was an enormous white noise. The pressure seemed to increase but remain constant, as though my body and the room itself were all simultaneously rising.

Due to the pressure, it was very difficult to the open the store's door. Of course I knew that whoever was behind the desk knew that I was standing in the foyer. Hearing the giant 'whoosh!' of the 25th street door being heroically pulled open by a customer alerted employees inside to look sharp. I use the word 'sharp' loosely. Colin VanAndervson, the owner, often did not raise his eyes from the wonderful boat video or car auction site he would customarily be engrossed in. He did, however, enjoy watching those customers who appeared unable to open the 25th Street door trying to open it. Some of them would try the locked door, which failed each time, and led to increased frustration. Some gave up and assumed we were closed; those with dogs inside were consistently persistent.

Inside the store Marcenda, who had broken up with me just days prior, rearranged the wares into ever more beautifully folded heaps on the merchandise tables. Raincoats, shoes, collars, hoods. She liked to count when gently arranging a pile. I watched her dark lips: *Uno, dos, tres.* I had never touched her in English.

Unfortunately, I did not see Colin behind the desk. His joviality at my shift's beginning was like vitamins and a B12 shot. Instead, Brittany, sometimes sweet but always sour - and often only the latter - stood with her back to me, looking through the large window at the dogs in the Little Dog Daycare room. Marcenda and I exchanged a glance as the dogs barked louder and more persistently than usual, which is what they did anytime someone looked into the daycare room through the window. The dogs, whatever their feelings for the Retreat, always wanted out.

I set my paper cup of coffee onto the turgid brown tile, marked with thousands of pockmarks from the overwhelming volume of urine, bleach, brooms, mops; and the incessant striking of canine toenails.

Brittany turned, gave Marcenda, then me, a sour smile, and sat her tall skinny frame behind the manager's computer at desk's center. She was closing for the night, which meant all four computers and three printers were in use, compiling the day's numbers. The credit-card receipt printer belched its ancient two-ply paper, whirring and sounding more as though it were tearing the paper to pieces than printing on it.

Brushing aside her short black hair, Brittany eyed the printer to her left in a suspicious way. The printer was spitting out hundreds of lists of receipts and I didn't know what else that would be useful for about twenty minutes before not being recycled. I could tell she was very nervous about all of the work she was asking of the printer, and hoping that it would not shit the bed. If it did, she would have to unplug it, plug in the backup printer, and resend all print jobs. Additionally, she might have to speak to Marcenda, even if only to tell her to move.

Marcenda had resumed her position as second in command behind the backup computer. She spun in her chair and elevated herself out of it, pushing down against the armrests so that she could peer into the daycare room. All the little dogs barked, and she returned her attention to the computer.

I spied the distinctive black and white fur of Brittany's dog, Eleanor, poking out beneath the desk. I knew she would be splayed in a comically awkward position, made horrible by her protruding vagina, beneath Marcenda's computer and the long desk.

Camille would be downstairs with the big dogs, mopping and filling water bowls and assuring herself that each bad dog - those not allowed to socialize with others - had a brief reprieve from their solitary runs in the daycare room, alone with her. She tossed a ball or tugged a rope as she walked between avenues and through the kitchen, emptying buckets into drains and bagging up the last of the shit; carrying food and beds and toys to dogs who were definitely in for the night. It was almost ten o'clock, closing and, therefore, bed time.

The runs were eight feet high and without a ceiling, save for four in the avenue directly off the kitchen. An avenue was what Colin called the lanes of runs, and each avenue was named after a New York avenue: Park, 5th, Broadway. I had been working at the Retreat for two years and still hadn't learned the names. I took the long way round if I had to give directions: The one closest to the kitchen; the middle one; the third one. Four of the runs off of the kitchen had a ceiling because Colin had nailed a great piece of plywood above them due to an energetic dog named Hercules.

Hercules, a Boxer, came daily to the NYCHR, and had become territorial about the place and too unpredictably mean to socialize. But he could also climb his way out of a run, which he did. The lane off the kitchen became known as Hercules' Run, because he would jump out and lounge about outside his run in the avenue until someone bothered to put him away again. He had scared hell out of several of us by just hanging out on top of the runs' bars, his front paws dangling over the side, looking menacing and dopey at once.

Marcenda sat looking at her computer. I glanced at her as I sipped my coffee and stood in the foyer, not yet at work. Ordinarily I'd have stood outside smoking, but I was early and had smoked three cigarettes already; and in the summer heat the sidewalk reeked of urine more powerfully than the foyer. Marcenda looked insufferable each time Brittany leaned over her to work on that computer for a moment. Brittany looked irate. And Brittany was a manager and Marcenda only a runner (s/he who retrieves dogs) so that settled that. In the United States, Brittany knew, you are how much you make. They had not spoken to each other since I had arrived, and I assumed it was the status quo and not a break in the action. No one liked listening to Brittany speak, because it was always only an opportunity for her to express biographical information, and none of it was of interest even to her, let alone to us.

The New York Canine Hedonistic Retreat closed at 10:00pm. This was more ballpark for Brittany, who arrived three hours early and never left before 11:00. Colin was irked not due to the wages, but that she acted as though she were doing the place some sort of favor. I suspected that Colin enjoyed having employees he found difficult to like, as though it gave him pleasure to suffer the lonely, illegal, weary, ugly employees he cajoled and bullied into endless conversation at the expense of work performed.

The paper coffee cup sat beside me, its heat leaving the softest circular pocket of condensation on the title. The light switch was turned to Off and glowed red in the darkness. Pressler Dog was not currently at the Retreat, but did happen by on occasion at his request.

Marcenda turned her head and looked across the room to Camille, who appeared after having ascended the stairs from Big Dog Daycare.

Camille carried two large black trash bags, full of the shift's waste. Brittany did not look up to smile or say Hi. She did not much make friends with the illegals. They couldn't give a *merde* is what I've heard.

I smiled and said Hello as she pushed open the door and swung the two bags in front of her body and set them on the foyer floor, allowing the door to close behind her. The foyer was instantly rife with the odiferous contents of the bags.

'Jonah, how *are* you, baby?' Camille, from the coast region of Ecuador, pronounced her J's something like a marriage of the SH and CH sounds. A sing-song quality in her cadence. I told her I was very well, '*Bien, bien, mucho,*' hoping she was less intent upon conversation, and more so on removing the trash bags to the street.

'Oh, so so, so so,' she said. 'You are...' She bent over, being taller than I, and brushed my hair tenderly. 'You are what? You are sleepy?' She made a bed of her hands and rested her head upon it, pouting out her bottom lip. She was the most attractive forty-year old woman I had known. 'You need woman.' Her dark hair rode waves of itself down her back, elegant against her light brown skin; lips rose pink, always smiling.

'And who better than you, Camille?' She laughed and flapped her hand at me - the hand not holding my coffee, which she's picked up from the floor - in that way females playfully slap a forearm (or near it) when you say something to make them laugh. She wore two pairs of sweatpants while on shift, one atop the other. This against Colin's vehement protestations and condemnations. Camille enjoyed the attention. She was forty and very pretty and called all of us 'Baby,' because she believed anyone under forty to be infantile in experience; unlimited in prospects; deserving of her affections.

I pretended to use my undershirt to wipe my nose with, and then pretended to leave the shirt there atop my nose, as though I preferred this; as though it were natural to me. I wanted to offer to remove the bags to the street myself, but did not want to infringe on her work, nor imply that I wanted out of our conversation.

'You too sleepy to work.'

'*Si si, much trabajo, mucho tranquillo.*'

'No *tranquillo*,' she said, laughing, '*CansAdo, cansAdo*,' teaching me the word in conversation.

'*Si, si, cansado-*'

'*CansAdo, cansAdo.*'

'*CansAdo.*' The only way to quell her was to pronounce the word correctly. And with enthusiasm. 'ConsAdo.'

A white male in a blue pin-striped suit opened the 25th Street door and entered the foyer with a firm step. His face betrayed immediate recognition of the garbage bag's contents. He offered brief eye contact with both of us, two inaudible Hellos, and stepped over the bags, between myself and Camille, to gain store access. Later, Brittany would scold Camille for being in a client's way. Marcenda had risen and was carrying a retrieved leash for the client's dog before the door came to rest behind his shiny black shoes. Camille offered the man a soft and extended 'Heeeeelllllooooo?' long after he had exited.

'And how is Marcenda?' She leaned against the door that never opened.

I smiled and shook my head, running my fingers over my nose so as to stop its ability to smell anything beyond my hands. I hoped she took the gesture to mean that I had a scratch.

'She's on shift with you, Camille. Haven't you spoken tonight?'

'And you, no?'

I broke a cigarette in half, and placed the pieces in either nostril, as I had seen soldiers do in war movies. Although we worked at the Retreat together, Marcenda and I had not had a conversation since we'd broken up.

Camille did not pause in chatter - the day's events, personal information about other employees - but made a face at me about the cigarette in my nose. The technique had worked in the past when I'd had occasion to use it - always and only at the NYCHR. The soft but pungent smell of tobacco; fields in the South. Tonight, however, it did little to keep the evening's odor away. She commented that the one up my nose was the healthiest one I'd have all day. I chuckled as she reached down and retrieved the coffee cup again, her Tshirt billowing. Conversation in the foyer required more vocal intensity than I cared for, due to the enormous white noise of the fan. I stared at the garbage bags, thinking that at some point I would be just in abandoning etiquette.

I wiped my finger across the sphere of moisture the cup left on the floor and instantly regretted it. I thought of disease rejoicing in water.

Somewhere on 25th Street, towards Broadway, echoed a sound that was either a dog shrieking or a black girl laughing. Over a dozen mid-sized moving vans blanketed both sides of the street. The vendors found parking spots if they arrived fifteen hours early for the Saturday/Sunday antique market in the parking lot across the street from the Retreat. Exhausted-looking men and women leant their grey faces against the windows, sleeping the public urban sleep in which the mind shuts off until a girl laughs or a horn wails. Dozens of struck matches littered the sidewalk outside the door.

'Hey brother Jonah man give me some,' Jimmy said as we high-fived and shook hands simultaneously. His long brown hair, knotted once, hung down his back in a long ponytail. From New Jersey, Jimmy drummed in a metal band. He adjusted the backpack slung on his right shoulder; he was on his way out, off the clock. 'What's the good word? How's the new job coming?' I had mentioned to Jimmy that I was picking up occasional temp shifts at Smear Bearns in Midtown; trying to find a way out of our current situation. 'Aw, Jonah man, you missed it, earlier man, so I was telling Britslit and Snarl about Japan.'

'Oh, right, how was it?' Jimmy called Brittany Britslit; and Karl was Snarl. His scrawny stature and relentless good humor let him get away with most anything.

'Snaggin, dude. First night, right? I'm fuckin jet lagged and broken so I get to the hotel and just pass. Wake up three in the a.m., right? My friends are back fuckin drunk and they got a hooker, this slim little thing, right? And she calls me Jimmy, 'cause they all call me Jimmy 'cause those fools can't pronounce my last name.' He pronounced his last name again, which sounded something like 'Jimmy.'

'Uh huh.' I nodded. Camille listened, drinking coffee, squinting her eyes and pursing her lips and tsk'ing and shaking her head in disapproval. I could not pronounce Jimmy's last name either.

'You are Meester gross, Meester Jimmy,' she said, slapping his bicep. 'You boys.'

'And so this girl, right? She's got this glittery dress on, right?' He posed with an intent to look sultry, as though he himself were wearing such a dress - and cleaning up in it. 'And she's sucking on a cigarette and the room's all dark and shit and they've all already fucked her and she says, "Fuck me, Jimmy. Fuck me."'

'And you did.'

'And I did, hayseed, I did.' He laughed and punched my belly playfully. I asked him if the papers in Japan had been carrying any of the stories about the threats to blow the hell out of-

'That place near Russia and China? Yeah, that was everywhere, dude. But you know I didn't read no papers, J-man.' I agreed that yes, I knew he had not read any papers.

25th Street was unsettling after nightfall. The 20/20 Club on Broadway the only open business. The endless pedestrians of New York walking past in gaggles. Those alone silent and staring the voided urban stare; the gaggles laughing and generally being loud for its own sake. Perhaps fifteen distinct masses of garbage lay on both sidewalks between Broadway and 6th Avenue. These were superbly avoided by all pedestrians, however inebriated. I felt pity for those parked outside the NYCHR who must exit their vehicles by way of our mass, surely the most awful on the block. In the neighborhood?

Cardboard everywhere, on both sidewalks, wrapped in plastic tape or just free-floating, kicked around by feet and vehicles and wind. I thought of all of the effort required to seriously clean a New York Street. It seemed an oppressive impossibility until one saw them doing it, from 5:00 to 7:00 each morning, with brooms and hoses, mops and buckets.

I imagined sheets of paper lifted singly and flying upwards, towards the closed windows of the top floors of the block's tallest buildings. Each piece of paper laying flat against each pane, held briefly in place before riding the resistance down and then away, out of sight. New crisp white sheets flying up from massive stacks of it in the street, one at a time, holding against the windows and riding back down.

Jimmy, on his way out, high-fiving me and slinging his backpack tightly over his shoulder, told Camille exactly what she should be doing with the garbage bags if she wanted to keep out the wolves, motioning with a thrust of his chin to Brittany, who was staring unflatteringly at Marcenda, who was asleep behind the desk.

'Marcenda is married, no?' Camille asked after Jimmy's departure.

'You know more than I, Camille.'

'Yes, she um, she will marry um, Meester Greg. He has two Weimaraners.' She pronounced the breed 'Wryer-wryer-er-er-er.'

'Mm. Yes. I know him.' I wasn't sure if I should react with cynicism or hearty good thanks, and so chuckled and asked when the wedding would be and at what court house. Of course Camille did not know, it being fourth or fifth-hand gossip, of which there was plenty at the NYCHR; though I largely remained out of any loop that was going around, as was my nature.

'I should clock in if I'm gonna pay the piper,' I said, holding out my open hand for the coffee cup. Camille smiled, pouted her lips; with both lips and eyes (and dark eyebrows) motioned to the door, to the street, her eyes glancing between the bags and myself and the street. She smiled. I obeyed.

4

'Of all the peasants I have come across in my roaming,' Tater waved his coffee cup extravagantly, much of the beverage washing over his hand, 'the most peasantish peasants are the French peasants. Only the tunnels and caves of Central Asia can equal a French village in unlimited peasantry.'

Mr. Tater Dola, tall and clean shaven, short blonde hair combed straight back, was only in the United States for the morning. That he had chosen to lunch with Jonah in Greenpoint was compassion incarnate. Tater would depart for Kabul in the afternoon. He thought he could outsmart Afghani (and so U.S.) immigration policy by flying from his native Poland to Afghanistan by way of the United States. Tater was intelligent and Jonah did not question this stratagem's validity - though privately he thought that it had little, if any; and that it was so paranoid it might be paranoid enough.

They were seated in what was known as Bea's Diner. The awning outside read Luncheonette Cafe, like hundreds of others in the city. All it really meant was, Here are burgers, sandwiches, coffee, fries. Bea owned the diner with her husband, Pieter, who operated the register before dark. Bea was short and wore a blue apron as uniform. Her white hair a full fluff of dandelion spores, not yet taken to the wind. She was the cook, waitress, bus-girl and dishwasher, overseeing the customers at the four booths running along the far wall, as well as the ten stools at the bar.

'What of the American peasant?' Jonah wondered how far from peasantry his mother's rural Maine upbringing had been. And what was the difference between peasant and hick and redneck? Any?

40

Tater winced with pleasure, biting into the hamburger Bea had just placed in front of him, the warm grease sluicing around his mouth, the warm yellow cheese soft on his tongue. Then he checked his watch. It had taken one hour by taxi from JFK to Greenpoint. It would be at least one hour returning. Jonah, who knew Tater as an administrator at Smear Bearns, was thankful for Tater's brief visits to Greenpoint; he thought it endearing, however inconsistent.

'The Americans have no peasants in an ideological sense. The American worships the idea of its small-time rural farmer, even if everything in government policy is done to impoverish these folk. Then there is her enormous and impoverished illegal population, not peasants in the traditional sense but. . . . The Americans are generally hicks, not peasants.'

'What is the difference?' Jonah smirked, not because of the conversation, but because Bea's coffee was strong enough to give him the stirrings of an erection and a bowel movement; a connection which he did not pursue further than acknowledging its existence.

'Peasants know they are peasants. Hicks might know they are hicks, but Hick is not a political or economic class. They are, in America, apolitical or depolitical.'

They were seated beneath the first community flag in the United States: Greenpoint's green and white, vertically-striped coat of arms: the lined and rudimentary image of a small city. Some of the local ladies' daughters had made it for Bea, and Bea had had Pieter hang it without delay.

'But Tater,' Jonah was contradictory, 'what of our millions-strong militias, seriously armed, in the Midwest?'

'This is only a sensible reaction to a government that so clearly is not interested in them or their interests and, moreover, causes them harm. It is not a political decision, in the customary sense, to arm one's self against an attacking force.'

'Are you afraid of Kabul?' Jonah changed the subject.

Tater scoffed. 'Six percent of Afghanistan has electricity now. I'll be fine. What is there to worry me? Daisy cutters? Cluster bombs? There's always the Comprehensive Test Ban Treaty!' Tater mocked, knowing that Jonah knew that his people stood alone in opposing the treaty, which would make all nuclear explosions unlawful. Jonah had no retort. 'I think cholera is coming back in Baghdad,' Tater continued, 'where I'll see if I can go after Kabul. Might as well make the imperial rounds, eh?'

'I wouldn't go to Baghdad with the best Kevlar vest the U.S. military could give me.'

'And you won't.' Tater was wicked. 'Did you read that Baghdad's sewage and drinking water are now synonymous?' Jonah had not. Tater supposed also that Jonah had not read of the Muammar brothers. Again, he was correct.

'I know, I know,' Jonah laughed, sheepish, dipping cooked potato bits into ketchup, 'I'm living under a rock.'

'No,' Tater said, 'only under the United States.' He shook his head as though Jonah had never heard of the *stan wojenny*.

Tater sneered at the pedestrians through the cafe's windows, while also smiling at the elegance of McGorlick Park in June. The park was alive with the sounds of children; the full colors of dozens of people reading, talking, watching. Tater's was not an easy disposition: love for all of humankind, derision for specific human beings. Though hate becomes, by nature, generalized.

'Greenpoint Poles,' Tater said, standing to ask Bea for more coffee before sitting again, 'are considered, in Poland, kind of . . . . painfully exotic. To some extent, flamboyant. To some extent, simply primitive. The quintessence of peasantry and rudeness.' He made a motion with his head, to indicate the wonderfully attractive Polish girls sitting at the bar. He lowered his voice. 'They are insulting everyone here.'

'In Polish?'

He nodded. Jonah shrugged. 'We are easy fare. The NYPD calls us marshmallows.'

'You're all from the USA sticks?'

'Quite. We are ruining - or least changing - their neighborhood. Their home. I wouldn't want it to happen to my hometown of three thousand, upstate. But I participate in it here.'

Tater shrugged, grinned. 'This is what a city is. Read your Jacques Ellul.' He sopped up egg yolk with toast. 'Anyway, most Poles think that Greenpoint is composed of Poles who simply did not - could not - amount to much in Poland.' He winced as a sports car, decorated in Polish decals, erupting dance music from its speakers - windows down - screeched from a stop to a start between Russell Street and Monitor Street, where it obeyed another Stop sign before screeching to a start again, tires hot. Tater was, by proxy, disgraced.

'That clumsy German-style one-metrum jack-hammer primitive non-melody disco shit!' His was a detailed critique. 'In Poland, that garbage is something like the poorest grade country music in the U.S.: a pseudo-music for total peasants.'

'Peasant is an insult for you.' Jonah saw no reason that this should be so.

'In our present context, yes. Though I am sure your hometown farming lads are fine peasants, as they come.' He was still sneering, staring out the window at where the car had been. 'That blasting garbage music is the archetypal sign of complete hillbilliness, redneckness, bad taste and primitiveness.' He sighed. 'The Poles here are so Polocentric. Like Joyce leaving Ireland only to write about it evermore. They leave Poland and then live as though they never wanted to leave.'

'You must have friends from Poland in Greenpoint.'

'None.'

Jonah laughed.

'Imagine all of American's most ridiculous hillbilly crowd moving to, say, Paris. This is how you arrive at Greenpoint.'

Jonah waved a hand towards the window and street beyond, to dismiss Tater's contempt for the loud sports car and general bravado of Greenpoint's Polocentric residents. 'Maybe it's just youth.'

'Jonah,' Tater stood, tossing cash onto the table, his cab honking its horn outside, 'I may be generalizing, unbalanced,' he donned his hat and shouldered his bag, 'unjust, abusive, not complying with the UN Declaration of Human Rights,' we walked outside, bidding Bea good day, 'but Greenpoint Poles become that: *Greenpoint* Poles. Not *Polish* Poles.'

Jonah pointed down Nassau Avenue to two new apartment buildings in the far distance, in Williamsburg. Cranes sat atop the tall structures, towering over the vicinity. With patriotism, he quoted George Washington. 'The gradual extension of our settlements will as certainly cause the savage, as the wolf, to retire; both being beasts of prey, tho' they differ in shape.'

'I prefer Jefferson.' Tater was short. Spitting his cigarette out the open cab window, he called after Jonah, wondering, 'Why are you still here? Hayseeds go back to the country.'

They shook hands through the open window before Tater departed, bidding 'adieu to the Athens of the East River.' Jonah did not know enough about the topic to think much either way, except that to be a Greenpoint Pole or a Polish Pole could not, by themselves, be much reason one way or another to think much of anything about anyone. But he had always been sentimental.

5

'What are you thinking about lunch?' Mr. Colin VanAnderv-son stood in the lobby of his pet services establishment, the New York Canine Hedonistic Retreat, holding he belly. His great height gave him leverage to stand behind the enormous plywood desk he'd built many years ago and survey the lobby, while alternately eating from one can of vegetable soup, and one can of chili, both unheated. Colin was a large man, and hungry; the cans' labels did not have time to grow moist in his hand before they were consumed.

'Awp.' Derik, Colin's employee and arguably best friend, gave Colin and the soups the crook-eye, but said nothing.

Ms. Brittany Delvone was downstairs in the kitchen, preparing the morning meal. She had agreed to work the AM and PM shifts in exchange for an invitation to Colin's home in Long Island, which only Derik and Jonah, of the NYCHR staff, had visited. That Brittany would be a guest in his home was upsetting to Colin, and her eagerness to be his guest confirmed for him his fear: that she desired him.

'The only time,' he told Derik, who was not listening, 'we've been alone together - and it was here at the Retreat, not my home - she-.' He paused, realizing Derik was not listening. 'Hey! Hey!'

'Awp. What? She made uncomfortable jokes about your body?'

'She touched my bicep!' He paused, allowing this to sink in. 'I predict she'll be playing with my pants and I'll have to flee my own home!'

'Jesus on speed, sit down, Colin.' Derik pushed off the floor with both cowboy boots, rolling his office chair into a collision with Colin's. Derik then stood, and began futzing with Colin's computer.

45

'Why the roll if you're just gonna stand anyway?' Colin asked, not expecting a response, which Derik did not offer. 'My second-sight is unquestionable!' he declared, standing and holding his large extended pointer finger up, to assert the point. 'When the Retreat had just opened, I was behind the desk when the prettiest goddamn Golden Retriever came in-'

'Yeah, yeah,' Derik leant over Colin to better control the mouse; Colin rolled away. 'That Joe Schmoe brought him in and you told Brittany-'

'It was Marcenda, not Brittany!' He again held up his finger but did not stand.

'And you told Marcenda that you'd get him hook or crook-'

'No!' This time Colin did stand. 'I said, "One day that dog will be mine!"'

'Jumping Jesus, Colin, I'm trying to show you something.' Derik gestured to the computer screen and the video of a boat pulling an enormous inflatable tube, and its passengers.

Colin was often predicting the future, or telling stories that featured him predicting the future. It was not as though he were bragging; only that he *had* done so, and thought it worth mention. He used his gigantic hands and mythic height to demonstrate the stories whose outcomes he had predicted.

The two were seated behind the enormous desk, which gave the impression of sturdiness. Colin considered it an immobile pack-mule. Derik did not know if the desk, which stretched the long width of the lobby, were real or synthetic wood. The desk was the center and base of the NYCHR, and also its mood and candor. Four computer screens (their hard-drives beneath the desk, collecting hair) glowed warmly. Small rectangles of sticky-paper covered the periphery of each screen, ink scrawled on the paper in many hues, shades and degrees of penmanship. Red, blue and vanilla folders lay scattered in fallen heaps and jumbles, disgorging their paper contents. A plethora of copy paper, used and unused, in singles or reams, was visible on top of and beneath everything. The used paper was adorned with dog's names and client's names and tax laws and menus printed from websites. Stacks of magazines, showcasing dogs adorned in snappy and adorable outfits, were shoved into corners and beneath other detritus. Boxes of pens everywhere; unless one were looking for one, in which case they lie hidden beneath folders and electrical cords and plastic Inboxes/Outboxes, themselves hemorrhaging documents. Three of the folders were exclusively for the menu collection, and were filled to spilling.

'Brooklyn 's in the house!'

Derik looked up from the computer to see Pam Cole standing just inside the glass doors in what he thought outlandishly puffy boots. They appeared to be lamb's wool and reached to her knees. Her pet, a small Maltese named Brooklyn, barked at Pam's feet repeatedly, with each falsetto yip her front paws leaving the tile as though to project her whole body into flight. Pam dropped the thin leash and Derik stood, knowing that Brooklyn would do as she did: wind her way around the displays of boots and treats and sweaters, and wait for the hallway door to be opened. Petite dogs such as Brooklyn simply scooted beneath the tables and racks, but Brooklyn opted for the maze. Which was okay by Derik, who adjusted his crotch.

Derik heaved open the door and Brooklyn entered. Derik, like all NYCHR employees, closed the door immediately behind him, shielding the doorway just in case Brooklyn - or some dog who had escaped and was cheesing it - tried to gain lobby access without leash supervision. Brooklyn walked to second door and waited. Yip yip. Derik unleashed her, opened the door just wide enough for her to sneak through without allowing any of the dogs already in daycare - a good dozen, who had gathered near the door and simply *had to know* what was going on out there - to escape. He stood, ran his eye over the alphabet Colin had etched on the wall seven feet high with a black crayon, and hung the leash on the hook beneath 'B.'

That Pam had said it, 'Brooklyn 's in the howw-ow-owse' had irritated the generally benign Colin and the not easily ruffled Derik.

Colin, as manager, was forced to make small talk with Pam while he gathered information and waited for her to go. Derik, not wanting any part of that scene, retreated into the daycare room, gleefully scooping up his favorite Cavalier, Anna Livia Plurabelle. He held her over his head, then let her torso rest on it, her four legs splayed about his eyes and ears. He called her sweet names and caressed her while, somehow, violently cursing and kicking and generally intimidating all of the other little dogs.

He said 'Hola' to Vashti, who was sitting with her feet on the chair, her Tshirt wrapped around knees and legs and torso. Vashti never spoke to Derik or Colin or Jonah; they figured because she was illegal, 'You know,' Derik had explained, 'since she's hot and foreign looking, like the rest of 'em.' That Vashti might know about as much Spanish as Derik did had never occurred to him; nor that she knew as much English.

Through the thick pane of glass Derik watched the blurred, underwater image of Pam Cole move across the lobby and exit. He set Anna down, with last kisses and promises of future reunion, and exited via the leash hallway, resuming his four-wheeled throne behind the long desk.

Colin opened his mouth and Derik held up a hand to silence him.

'She's not a prostitute,' Derik said.

'She's around town. No doubt about it.' For Colin, expressing an opinion was a statement of fact. X movie is the best of the year. X place is no place to vacation. Girl X is worth an expensive dinner, while Girl Y you treat to hot-dogs in the park nearest her residence.

'Those boots?' Colin urged. 'The Sunday morning mini-skirt in Chelsea where it's only our dog palace and the bagel shop open until noon?'

'Blah. Ahp.' Derik was dismissive.

'She's on the job at this moment. She didn't want Brooklyn to see Mommy doing the dirty with strange men, so to the Retreat.'

'And Christ sawed off my foreskin, Colin. Find hard evidence she's selling ass, and I'm buying dinner.'

'Speaking of which, what are you thinking for lunch?'

*

Brittany opened her eyes and looked through the windows above the kitchen sink, and through the green daycare room beyond the windows, and beyond the dogs in the daycare room, and saw a warm place free of urine, hair and barking. She blinked and shook her head, realizing that the cold water she was running over her finger was cold to a painful extent. She had cut the finger on the lid of a soft food can. Subsequently, she had made what she called An Executive Decision that no dogs would receive soft food today.

Brittany knew what all lunch preparers - and not every employee was awarded the responsibility - knew: that it was the most time-consuming and, consequently, most rewarding task at the Retreat. Firstly, it did not involve spending time with dogs. Colin had declared that the meal preparer was not to 'Touch, play, or even save the life of any dog until the feeding is over! Unless it's my dog, for whom you will sacrifice all.' Colin proclaimed most new rules and regulations sporadically and spontaneously, and as only a few of the staff would be present for any given declaration, there was little uniformity in the execution of his wishes; or even awareness of them. Word about the singularity of the meal preparer's task had gotten around mostly due to Jonah, who enforced Colin's decree with satisfied resolve.

As more NYCHR dogs ate breakfast than dinner, the morning feeding was the day's major task. The meal preparer was also responsible for the administering of medications, oral or otherwise. The medication was something Colin only heeded for two or three days at a time, usually after some dog had received the wrong pill or ointment. Derik and Jonah thought he rather enjoyed the opportunity to prove that his declarations were warranted, whatever consequence to the un/over-medicated pup(s).

Colin asked, without averting his gaze from the computer screen, who was on shift downstairs with the big dogs that night. Derik squinted to read the schedule, taped to the thick glass wall, in so doing spotting a lonesome and abandoned looking Anna Livia Plurabelle. 'Jimmy and Camille' he shouted to Colin as he bounded towards the hall, his heart pounding at Anna's isolation. Colin had already forgotten he'd asked a question, never mind what the question was. His attention was on online auctions for Pontiac GTOs, which he was scheming to purchase, fix, and sell profitably.

'Vashti!' Derik hollered, squeezing his body into the daycare room through the doorway, using both feet to ward off potential escapees, including The General, whose bassy bark sounded like 'Booo' ricocheting off of the concrete walls. 'Vashti, why is Anna Livia sitting all alone?' Picking her up, he rubbed his stubbly face on her malodorous and soft belly. 'Love her! Love her!' He set Anna in Vashti's lap and exited through the third door, opposite the door to the leash hallway.

Finding himself in the red room - more of a maroon, he thought - he eyed the small cages stacked on top of each other and side by side, looking for a favorite. Finding none, he walked further back to where the full-sized runs housed big dogs too old or sick to walk downstairs; or dogs just groomed and awaiting departure. Derik looked in, to be sure no one was sitting in excrement or chewing its new hairdo to pieces. He liked to see Chan, the groomer, make bank on his tips.

*

Brittany watched through the window in the kitchen door as Lionel set water bowls, filled to spilling, inside the dog's runs, being sure to use his body as a shield against escape. Unless it were a warm summer day, the only dogs that ever finished their water did so by knocking the bowl over and jumping around in the resulting puddle. These were usually the dogs who greatly disliked confinement in the run, and let it be known with wild behavior. Consequently, they spent more time in their runs than did the dogs who just hunkered down and suffered it quietly.

Brittany, through a series of delaying tactics and obscure, trivial tasks - all of which she'd picked up from observing Jonah - was attempting to absorb the entire morning with the meal preparation. If successful, her lunch break would end just before the PM staff came on shift, when she could flee the daycare room for an even longer break no one questioned because the dust from punching-in was still fresh on their hands. Brittany wanted to sit behind the long desk with Colin and Derik - like a manager (which is what she was) always did.

Derik and Colin were pretty much on lunch break the entire shift, with brief interruptions to chat with clients about eye drops or anal glands.

Brittany scooped more dry kibble into the silver metal bowl, wet it with cold water from the tap, drained the water, and poured it into a paper feeding tray labeled 'Peeps.' She tried to imagine the scenario about to play out, of her joining Colin and Derik upstairs. She tried to envision what it would be like, what they would say, so that she would have something quick and funny to say in response. She should have known, but did not, that Colin paid enough attention to her that she would be unable to complain that he was not listening; but no more. Brittany's best jokes were slanted against the illegals.

Jonah had wondered aloud to Colin, weeks back, why the immigrants - who were very obviously mistreated by Brittany, however ineffective the mistreatment proved to be - did not file legal or at least serious complaints with Colin about her. 'Jonah,' Colin explained, 'none of these sorry bastards could speak enough of the language to lodge a tennis ball.'

'Lob, you mean, Colin.'

'Your ass I did.'

*

Colin, while bestowed with the gift of gab, never wasted it on fools. Even the attractive female sort. This meant Holly Hertle, and her blonde beehive hairdo, too. Colin maintained a professional distance with Holly, tempered by his natural goodwill and frankness.

'And how long is Henrietta going to be with us?' he asked, entering the information into the computer database; a database which, he claimed, was designed using software developed for U.S. penitentiaries.

Derik, not smitten with Holly Hertle's beehive either, escorted Henrietta, a large collie, downstairs to big dog daycare. He paused a moment in the downstairs viewing area, between the kitchen and Bad Dog Alley. Remembering that Henrietta had a history of provoking fights, instead of a left he took a right, to Bad Dog Alley, and the Do Not Mix dogs.

He moved with Henrietta beyond the large standing sinks - just in case the two sinks upstairs broke - full of fifty pound bags of kibble and boxes of cleaning supplies. The wide window that looked into the viewing area was permanently curtained, for the obvious reason that the dogs housed back there left their cells about as often as Jose Padilla.

The Do Not Mix dogs were the only dogs consistently walked at the Retreat. Although some employees just had the dogs do this business in the open floor near the standing sinks. The open floor, painted black, was cracked and demented with urine and bleach and shit.

Recently, in what Derik had called 'One of his fits of being tired of paying people to sit around drinking coffee with him,' Colin had declared he was 'Now taking the whole dog-walking thing seriously.'

The most strenuous activity on the job was the constant up and down of the stairs. All twenty-three, Derik thought, gritting his teeth, thinking of his walk back up. Plus, he thought, it was never debonair to walk 25th Street, holding an enormous and transparent bag of shit.

Particularly past the somewhat highbrow 20/20 Club at block's east end. This was permissible and hidden in the darkness and obscurity of 24th Street, on the NYCHR designated walking route between 6th Avenue and Broadway.

Derik was tired, and grateful Henrietta had only one name. Those with two confused him when hanging the leash in the hallway. Was Lord Peabody L or P? What about The General? Why was Jonah, he thought, the *only one* to take advantage of the definite article?

The leash hallway stretched the entire length of the building, and ended with stairs, down to an ever-locked door that reached big dog daycare. Midway down the hall an enormous fan, completely covered in black dust and moist filth, blew air from the hallway into the alley between the Retreat and the office building next door. The fan served no purpose anyone could ascertain - or trick Colin into explaining - save for sucking the overnight employee's cigarette and/or marijuana smoke out and away, in the silent, dark hours.

'Now Henrietta eats twice a day, with two snacks, but you already know that.' Holly laughed a dry, thankless laugh. Colin swallowed and grinned like he was charming a mother.

'Two snack minimum!' he said. Pretending to spoil the dogs would get him everywhere.

Derik pulled from Henrietta's overnight bag a small brown bear, and stuck a white label to it. 'And that one she likes best at bedtime,' she said. Colin coughed to alert Derik, who looked up, smiled, removed the label and affixed it to the overnight bag - as though it had been his intention the entire time - and nodded at Holly's instruction, balancing eye-contact between her dark blue oval eyes and the paper he was pretending to take notes on.

'Right, bear at bedtime,' he said. Pulling an orange turtle from Henrietta's bag, he improvised. 'And if I remember right, this she likes at lunch, no?' Colin smirked; Holly laughed and clapped her hands in delight.

After Holly's departure, Derik affixed white labels to each of Henrietta's possessions. These were then crammed back into the overnight bag and, with great strength and flexibility, the bag was somehow forced into one of the lockers in the back.

Colin had been lenient (which for him is downright reckless) with the labeling process for some time, even after the label decree.

'From this day forward,' he had said, rising with a meaty finger to the heavens, 'all possessions will be labeled and lockered, and when the dog goes home these labels will be removed and the toys rubbed into the floor and thrown around a bit so that the client believes they were played with.'

'Down to the last flea-ridden blanket and stray slobbery treat?' Jimmy had asked - though he couldn't give two damns and three Jimmys about tasks, extra or otherwise, is what he told Jonah.

'And each goddamn kibble,' Colin said. 'Literally.' His icy (serious) tone - wholly uncharacteristic of Colin - had pretty well excused everyone from the day's impromptu meeting about labels. Colin had had to hastily call everyone back and explain that, literally, he did not mean each kibble.

This decree had been effective for about a month, the locker/possession technique very successful, before the staff - and Colin - got bored with the procedure. Unhappily, a host of clients had been complaining recently concerning unreturned or misreturned items, to an extent that Colin had been serious and straight-faced for an entire afternoon, and the whole Retreat felt like it'd never seen the sun. Which of course the entire basement hadn't.

Colin and Derek were admiring online pictures of automobiles they wished to achieve coitus with, when Officer Hunky waddled into the lobby, his owner, Brock Myrol, holding the door. Derek waited, seated, for Hunky to reach the hallway door, which he did with neither excitement nor dread. Despite his sixty pounds, Hunky stayed with the little dogs, upstairs, due to his lack of 'playful joviality.'

'He likes to play,' Brock began reciting to Colin, who heard it every Saturday, 'but not too rough. He doesn't have the playful joviality of those big guys downstairs.' Brock's hair was combed so tightly to the left, and shellacked so thick, Colin felt he could reach out and grab it, like an object, and remove it from Brock's scalp.

Finding his hand reaching out to do just that, Colin quickly averted the hand into the treat basket, which sat on the desk's surface. Lacking a dog to throw it to, he tossed the treat into the air, opened his mouth looking upward, and caught it. Brock, being a regular customer, had seen and even been invited to participate in Colin's dog food antics, though he always declined. Colin thought Brock a prostitute, as well. Derek figured he sold weapons internationally to underground militias. If either had done a quick Internet search, they would have found was a top advisor to New York Mayor Edward H. Gerdemann, currently inhabiting City Hall.

The little dogs, greeting Officer Hunky at the door with snouts sniffing, were certain to warn him, with declarations frequent and shrill, that just because he was a big fat schlub didn't mean that he could come onto their turf in their territory and tell them what was what; and if that was what he thought he was sorely misinformed. Hunky, not giving much of a damn what the little dogs had to say, sat in the far corner licking the, presumably salty, floor.

Derik, after waiting out Brock's small talk and finally, his departure, resumed his seat and labeled Hunky's possessions. He taped a list of the items onto Colin's computer's screen - not knowing where Colin was disappeared to, but pretty sure it involved flushing something - before depositing the possessions in a locker, the number of which he added to the list. Colin, who had returned looking pleased with himself, emptied Hunky's treats into the garbage can until he thought it looked as though three weeks worth of treats had been consumed. Hunky's stay at the NYCHR would be, miracles and Camille aside, treatless.

'There is a thin line here,' Colin advised Derek, 'between pretending to have given a dog too many treats, and pretending to have given it too few.'

Derek grunted in recognition and resumed the playing of a boat video on his computer screen. Colin, reluctantly, turned away from the video and began entering the notes for Officer Hunky's stay in the database. These notes would be a part of the Dogs Still To Leave / Dogs Staying Over lists, which were ideally given to each employee at the beginning of shift, but rarely made it to a successful print job. Colin's notes for Officer Hunky read,

> feed am/pm 1.5 cups water. owner says to let food sit in water for 10 minutes before serving. let's save a food tray and just put the food in the water bowl. going home on the 19th. THIS DOG MUST HAVE A BATH BEFORE CHECK OUT OR I, COLIN, WILL HARM WHICHEVER MANAGER WAS ON SHIFT FOR DEPARTURE and the 19th looks to be a Saturday so BRITTANY, this means YOU!!! this dog's owner bitches like me on a diet if the dog is not clean! dog likes to sit in corner, lick piss. shake it every 30 minutes to make sure it's not dead.

Another note from Colin, beneath the above entry in the database, from Hunky's previous Retreat stay, read,

> THIS OWNER IS A FUCKING NIGHTMARE!!!! DO NOT TAKE RESERVATIONS!! DO NOT LET DOG STAY HERE EVER!!! COLIN HAS SPOKEN!

It was not uncommon for Colin to permit previously barred clients from returning to the Retreat, given that a few weeks had passed and he had forgotten the altercation. There was little he cared enough for that could stir a grudge within him; which is not to say that he was unfeeling.

The walkie-talkie on the desk cracked and Brittany was heard asking, 'What does Countess Ivanova eat AM?' Colin, his eyes glazed in the tension between typing more notes, picked up the device without looking at it and flung it towards Derik, who switched it off and set it down without interrupting his gaze from the boat video.

Colin had purchased the walkie-talkies to spare everyone the effort of running the twenty-three stairs to the basement and back; even for trivial things like what Countess Ivanovna ate for breakfast. 'The important thing is what are you thinking for lunch?' Derik grunted.

Brittany, standing over the sink in the cold kitchen, continued to overlook that Colin had never evidenced much care as to whether dogs were fed and medicated accurately. 'Derik's good with the dogs,' Colin had told her on the phone the night before, flattery getting him everywhere, 'but I don't trust him to the do the feeding and medication properly. That's what I need you for tomorrow.' Insulting Derik's dog-caring abilities was easy, and avoiding working the Sunday morning shift behind the desk with Brittany was the thick white icing to Colin's Sunday morning pastry.

A further *intended* use for the walkie-talkies was the ability for the front desk to see a client entering, and quickly relay the information to the downstairs daycare employees. With a head start, these employees could be sure to have the dog out in daycare and not in a run, in the event that the owner wanted to see their pup at play, which was not often. Nobody but Colin, however, felt comfortable hurriedly picking up the black device and shouting instructions into it within the three seconds between the client being out of earshot (in the foyer) and within. Further, nobody downstairs much cared for carrying around the clunky apparatus. Those who fashioned loose-fitting pants would see them dragged from the knees to the ankles with a heavy walkie-talkie clipped to the waist. Mostly, the downstairs device sat on the silver table in the large green daycare room, untended, transmitting sounds and messages to an audience of attentive dogs, whose ears twitched with a confused comprehension at the not entirely strange sounds from the black thing on the table. Those nearest the table would look around suspiciously as they listened, as though wary of who else would hear. Or see?

Above the sink hung the Feeding List and the Medication Sheet, two clipboards hanging on nails. Brittany glanced at them occasionally as she rolled pills into balls of wet food, placing them in the appropriately-labeled food tray. The sink was constantly running during meal preparation. Three or four hours of a light cold drizzle. Beside the sink sat ten cans of wet food, their open lids jagged and menacing. She rubbed hungover eyes, setting the four indispensable feeding tools down: can opener, fork, one-cup measuring cup, plastic bowl; the latter to mix the dry kibble with water, which was then drained. Brittany believed it augmented the odor and made it more palatable for the dog. Pressler Dog had told Jonah that this was not so, but who ever believed a Pressler Dog?

Derik, bored with the internet, was pretending Anna Livia Plurabelle was an alien enveloping his face. Her soft belly felt delicious on his face, rough with stubble. Anna looked confused, the brown swirls in her white fur looking comically misaligned, as though she were laughing at something that made her very sad.

This sadness suddenly changed to terror when she heard the thunder of Colin's pounding on the daycare window with his massive closed fist. All of the little dogs, frightened - save for Officer Hunky, who was still licking the yellow floor at his front paws - immediately began barking at Colin, letting him know that if he thought if could come in here and tell them what was what. . . . 'Make sure that dog's not dead,' Colin shouted, pointing to the corner he could not see from his vantage point. 'Officer Hunky.'

'He's licking the floor,' Derik shouted, the terror on Anna's face turned to adoration for Derik, her savior.

'Okay, good. What are you thinking for lunch?'

*

Derik held his stomach and checked his watch. 10:30am. He had coffee-gut, and the buttery croissant was not making for good company, either. 'Bought a third cat last night, me and Leora,' he said, leaning back in the chair to better extend his legs on the desktop. 'It's a ragdoll. We named him Mighty.'

'I'm thinking burgers.' Colin was not to be deterred or distracted. 'You know if you're thinking anything at all over there? Regarding lunch?' He stretched, dominating the five-wheeled chair with his size, yawning and patting affectionately the mild swelling of his belly.

Downstairs, Brittany saw red as she slit her thumb opening a new can of wet food. This was the common hazard involved with feeding; the other being the dog who *did not want* to receive medication. The blood dripped in large ovals into the silver sink; the smell of rust comingling with kibble, gelatinous wet canned food, and the musty dryness of dog hair; some of the latter in the form of dust.

She held the liberally bleeding thumb beneath a cold stream of water as Derik gracelessly kicked open the door and entered, preceded by Duchess Didi, a sweet and hyperactive Pit Bull. Brittany smiled unevenly by way of greeting, so that Derik cold tell the cold water was more uncomfortable than the wound. Holding Didi tightly by her purple leash - lest she knock over every open container of kibble, and the refrigerator besides (she was a *strong* Pit) - Derik leant over the sink to inspect the wound, setting down a lunch menu. He frowned slightly, as if to say, 'Unfortunate, but nothing to raise alarms about.'

Brittany, studying the menu, made a face: *Little too early for lunch, no?*

Derik responded with a shrug: *Colin's hungry.*

After depositing Didi in a run, he received Brittany's lunch order and returned upstairs, two-stepping up the black steps in his brown cowboy boots.

Colin and Derik were studying the menu with scholarly scrutiny when Brittany appeared behind the desk, holding pieces of the Feeding List, which were pocked and speckled with food, water, ink, blood, medication. A fist to her hip, she reported, 'Emir Akerson vomited, then ate it and vomited again. By the time I got over there with a mop, Vicar Joslin had eaten that. Just fyi. And what are we feeding Countess Ivanovna?' She exhaled from the corner of her mouth.

'You want any Tejas sides with yours?' Colin asked, holding aloft the menu. She shook her head, knowing sides from the Texas BBQ & Grill would only further frighten a stomach already busy considering a Texas BBQ & Grill hamburger. Colin referred to the place as Tejas - soft 'j' - in deference to the Latino population at the NYCHR, who never much ordered lunch anyway.

All three of their heads turned at the whoosh of the 25th Street door being opened. Brittany quickly took her leave at the sight of Ms. Caroline Button, who had arrived two hours early to retrieve her pup, Early, the Golden Retriever whose blanket Derik was currently grinding into the floor with Colin's size 15s, so that the blanket looked as though it had been used by Early and not sat folded and useless in a locker for the last two months.

Happily, the duo had confronted such a situation before. By the time Ms. Button gained lobby access, Derik had - with an agile flick of his boot - kicked the blanket beneath the desk. Colin then used his long legs to push it further from desk's center. Derik gave Ms. Button a quick 'Hello' with a wave, before ducking under the desk with a garbage bag, concealing the blanket within, and cheesing it through grooming and to the back, where he could conspicuously cram all of Early's possessions into the garbage bag together. Colin, to make small talk, asked Ms. Button if she wanted to order anything from Tejas. Ms. Button demurred, with a face that said she'd rather order from the Retreat's own kitchen.

*

Colin rubbed his hands together, partly to dry the soft patches of barbecue sauce still clinging to them, and partly in anticipation of eating something beyond the burger and fries he had ordered and consumed. Brittany's untouched hamburger was close to becoming Colin's; and touched.

Brittany, wiping kibble dust from her forearm, figured she'd better reapply the thumb bandage, which had bled through and was soaked in water anyway; peppered and dusted with food, pill dust and hair. The juxtaposition of preparing dog meals while being extremely hungry was unpleasant to most Retreat employees, Brittany not excluded.

Their meals finished, Derik and Colin (the latter having finished Brittany's, subsequently ordering her another) slouched in their chairs behind the desk, legs splayed before them, bellies puffed and cradled in their warm hands. Colin, with one enormous finger, was pounding the day's notes into the database. He wanted to finish the notes by 2:00pm, so that the PM shift would be fully informed and he could leave early. He had plans for an evening of grilling in his Long Island backyard.

The NYCHR PM shift began at 2:00pm. The 2:00 - 3:00 hour consisted of daycare employees assuming their positions in the two daycare rooms. Meanwhile the managers and runners - both AM and PM - sat behind the desk with the intention of relating particular and timely information; as well as which lies to tell each client. In practice, the hour consisted of Colin yucking it up with jokes he'd been telling Derik - or whoever else was around - all morning.

Colin worked on the Dogs Still To Leave list, as it had urgent precedence over the Dogs Staying Over list, given that dogs staying over would not have an owner to deal with during the coming shift. However off-topic Turnover became - and Colin telling stories about his childhood nemesis Fat Philes was certainly off-topic - the Retreat was one big quiver of uninformed strangeness without it.

Dog: Jonkheer Reedy.

Breed: Australian Cattle Dog. Black/White/Gray/Brown.

Client: Zosi Zosima Reedy.

In Date/Time: 06/16/06. 7:30am.

Out Date/Time: 06/16/06. 4:00pm.

Special Instructions: feed am/pm. This dog eats shit. Everyone knows it. Karl, I'm looking at you here. If this dog gets picked up with a shit-eating grin, it won't be the only one in the house. Client has complained many times about the shit eating. Blarf. Sheieimbti20w49y5imhoe5im5eb5mb094mb0w94mgw23i 5hoi3ign5in4win4ignjntkhsn. No more Tejas. Fuck Tejas.

With great care to move without swiftness, and without moving his body, Colin turned his head towards Derik, his hand gently resting atop the swell of belly. 'You, us, coffee?'

'No!' Derik grunted, adamant.

'Here's the tip purse.' Colin, moving too hastily for the comfort of the swell, tossed the blue purse in Derik's direction, the purse landing somewhere between the two, on the floor, sending a puff of hair and dust upwards.

'Gluuuuuuggggggggggg.' Derik removed a twenty-dollar bill and, with heroics, exited onto 25th Street, holding his belly.

Dog: Tubby Short.

Breed: Staffordshire Terrier. Brown/White.

Client: Luci Coco Short.

In Date/Time: 06/16/06. 8:00am.

Out Date/Time: 06/16/06. 6:30pm.

Special Instructions: feed am/pm. Tubby eats Retreat employees for breakfast lunch dinner. (Bet she couldn't handle fucking Tejas though!) DO NOT MIX THIS DOG! DO NOT TOUCH THIS DOG! He was bouncy and treat-eating when brought in by owner. Was put into a run on Broadway by Derik with blanket and pillow. Blanket and pillow were torn to pieces before Derik could realize he and I didn't give a damn! ONLY A MANAGER CAN TOUCH THIS DOG! If I have to fill out workman's comp papers because someone who is NOT A MANAGER touched this dog, they will feel my Tejas wrath! Make sure owner thinks blanket and pillow made it through most of the day, until Tubby just couldn't wait to see her dear cigarette-smelling owner and ripped 'em up in anticipation. Blurf.

Colin massaged his pointer (typing) finger with his thumb, staring not out the 25th Street windows, but at the dog beds that lay for sale on the shelves before the windows. Any employee who had worked an Overnight shift knew the siren's call of four 2' x 4' dog beds jammed together on the cold NYCHR floor.

Dog: Chairman Ziegler.

Breed: Labrador Retriever. Yellow.

Client: Remy Zielger.

In Date/Time: 06/16/06. 8:00am.

Out Date/Time: 06/16/06. 9:30pm.

Special Instructions: feed am. The Chairman sometimes gets dio. Rrhea, that is! Has owner provided food in red bag Bitch owner left with $1 advance tip. Bitch said 'Make sure it doesn't get lost or'. Then Bitch paused, thinking hard. Then said 'Or dirty or something.' I, Colin, hereby decree that any NYCHR employee can fuck this Bitch any which way he or she knows how. Karl, I'm looking at your here, pardner. Make it as uncomfortable and unenjoyable as we all know you can. (Which you know he will, sinners! This parenthesis note by Derik, bitches! Leora 4ever!)

Dog: Envoy Fitzwater.

Breed: Papillion. Black/White.

Client: James Speakes.

In Date/Time: 06/16/06. 9:15am.

Out Date/Time: 06/16/06. 7:00pm.

Special Instructions: do not feed. This dog is here for a BATH ONLY! Envoy can play with the little dogs before but NOT AFTER HIS BATH. Chan isn't washing dogs and squeezing anal glands for nickels, after all. Fucking Tejas! I, Colin, hereby forbid anyone to suggest ordering Tejas while I am in the building! Gurgle gurgle blurf.

Derik, returning from 25th Street's sunshine, set down two paper coffee cups and deposited the change from the twenty-dollar bill into the tip purse, accounting for the transaction on the Tip Accountability sheet. He sat down heavily in the gray office chair and, in unison with Colin, sighed with two hands caressing a troubled belly. Derik's flatulence against the chair sounded like a cell phone's vibration in a pocket.

There were three garbage bins - green, gray and black - behind the desk, for the ample waste created throughout the day. Colin needed to find a receipt he had tossed out hours earlier when he had wanted to shoot a basket and the receipt had been the first crumple-able object in the vicinity. Failure to find the receipt would mean manual changes to various files and lots of unnecessary but inescapable explanations to Brittany, who kept eyes on the monies and liked explanations from Colin; and the power they seemed to afford her.

The green trash bin was becoming the inverse of the gray bin, which had been dragged over from the wall by Colin's size 15s. Whatever in the gray bin which had been close to falling over the overflowing rim was now languishing on the bottom of the almost empty green. 'The first shall be last and the last shall be in the green bin!' Colin shouted, presumably to Vashti, who sat in the empty little dog daycare room staring numbly at the walls, unhearing; or perhaps to Chan and Derik, who were joking around in the grooming area.

Either way, he was shouting a joke that only he could understand - and shouting it through thick glass to people who were unaware of being spoken to. Colin laughed, regardless, setting Tejas wrappers and crumpled papers and ketchup packets (some empty, some not) and napkins (used and not) from gray to green bin. This beautiful Tejas mess was covered by the clean and heavy deposit of 180 sheets of paper atop it, these due to Colin's accidental printing of 200 Grooming Lists, instead of 20. The whirr of the printer often became as common, as imperceptible, as the narcotic hum of a refrigerator. The thought caused Colin to remember Jonah's comment that the wonderful hum of a fan was like someone from really far away saying 'It's okay, it's okay, it's okay,' over and over again, from really far away.

Sticky notes and sugar packets and coffee cups and papers (crumpled, folded, origamied into guns and tanks and footballs - Derik's work) and empty pastry wrappers were transferred from gray bin to green. Colin had already largely abandoned the idea of finding the receipt, given that we wasn't about to open up each crumpled object and have a look, and so was moving trash from one bin to the other for no particular reason save that no other distraction had chanced upon him.

He looked up and ceased the garbage transference when Brittany, having ascended the stairs, paused at desk's end, waiting for his attention.

'Vicar Joslin vomited the vomit he'd eaten from Emir Akerson, and also had diarrhea. Marquise Nessen shoved her food right through her run door and Notary Salinger ate it, as well as his own food. And Salinger eats owner provided food and Nessen eats purple Wellness, so I guess Salinger should be fine unless he's allergic to something not on my list.' She held aloft her stained and crumpled Feeding List, and stared at Colin's gut long enough that Colin could not tell if she were lost in thought or actually openly staring at his gut. Or his cock? 'What are we feeding Countess Ivanovna?'

'Coffee?' Colin asked her, offering his untasted cup to her. Brittany shook her head. Colin was wondering what in the hell they *did* feed the Countess when an hysterical cackling laugh from Chan drew Brittany's attention to the grooming area, where Chan was urgently calling her over.

Chan, whose family had escaped Vietnam in the late 60s, told hilarious stories, even if one could not understand any of the words he spoke. As most of his stories involved dogs, one only needed to watch his series of gestures - often using whichever dog he were grooming as a prop - to ascertain that he was telling a story about having cut a dog's hair too short; or how Vietnamese whores knocked out their own front teeth to better facilitate fellatio.

Dog: Dumny Salif terHorst.
Breed: Great Dane. Brown.
Client: Ron terHorst.
In Date/Time: 06/16/06. 7:45am.
Out Date/Time: 06/16/06. 10:00pm.
Special Instructions: Owner says Salif is a little nervous around other dogs, and should be given many breaks. Read: if this dog so much as sneezes near another dog, make it a DO NOT MIX immediately. The size of this dog makes ME question more than just my masculinity, and I'm COLIN! (Note from Derik, sluts: What else are you questioning besides your masculinity, Colin? God? Existence? What the huge amount of meat we could glean from this pup would be worth in Chinatown?)

Dog: Champ Dufrenoy Siewert.
Breed: Terrier. White/Brown.
Client: George Siewert.
In Date/Time: 06/16/06. 7:00am.
Out Date/Time: 06/16/06. 5:00pm.
Special Instructions: Colin says fuck this dog. Colin says feed this dog Tejas. Seriously, if this dog leaves the Retreat with dingleberries from shit-dancing there will be problems. If dog shits in his cage - and we all KNOW he's gonna! - DO NOT LET HIM DANCE IN IT! Take him to the 20/20 Club if you have to but DO NOT LET HIM DANCE IN HIS OWN SHIT OR ANYONE ELSE'S!!!!! Has toys in locker #....

Colin paused to ask Derik in which locker number Champ's possessions were located. Through the thick glass behind him, he saw Derik dancing around the pillar in little dog daycare, dipping and cradling and altogether fondling Anna Livia Plurabelle, who looked transfixed, like a penitent; or a martyr.

...Well Derik put the possessions away so Derik, at Turnover remember to tell someone the locker number. If I have to shake lockers empty to find this dog's possessions I'll dance in my own shit and ask Derik to partner me.

If Countess Ivanovna was fed Wellness or Iams or Nutro, Colin was not made aware of it. June was thrilling on 25th Street, and the cigarette he'd taken from Jonah - who had just come on shift - tasted like a transcendental fog on an unknown river in an unknown glade. High above, Colin heard the whirr of helicopters, which he preferred to the barking inside.

6

The promptly scheduled and much promoted (by the organizers, at least) street protest opposing a number of ongoing wars and occupations, had the blessing of the largely intolerant Gentle Administration. Also, the good wishes of any representative who wanted to receive a legitimate vote in New York State in the future. (They had polled the people with extraordinary speed.)

This public approval was astonishing from an administration that had sacked 110,00 United States Postal Service employees for signing a petition seeking to prohibit the *macabre* Fallujah stamp; incidentally, making it an instant collector's item.

The Gentle approval came, plainly, with its conditions.

The administration, using a man so inside that he had been special advisor to both President Gentle and New York's Mayor Gerdemann, sent Brock Myrol to politely ask the Mayor to move the thing to the Bronx, please, we don't need that ruckus here. We've got tickets to Lincoln Center and the wife isn't coming. And, Myrol further pressed the Mayor, the administration was prepared to summon the National Guards of New Jersey, Delaware and Connecticut, as well as other *Foederati* (and maybe even New York, too, if the Governor were feeling patriotic) to assist with the enormous number of anticipated arrests.

The Mayor, sighing and gazing at portraits of predecessors hanging in his office, suggested the long dormant asylum on Roosevelt Island, among other locales, as a possible detention center. Myrol grimaced and chuckled, scotch in hand, saying one administration official had been heard yearning for the days of Blackwell Island's holding cells.

Mayor Gerdemann, with a smile, entrusted all of the city's resources to Brock to help the administration in pursuit of law.

Privately, Myrol was scared shitless of detention centers, if you wanted to know the truth about it. He had seen many, and they were always unpleasant in every conceivable manner but the most important: they remained under control.

Also privately, Myrol was concerned for his mistresses, as many of them had informed him that they were planning to participate in the demonstration, and the things that might happen to one at a detention center were things Myrol preferred to save for himself and his mistresses at home. Also, he did not need some New York cop calling him every ten minutes to clear some other broad who used his name to get out of the tank.

With these considerations in mind, Myrol did something he would only do one other time in his career, and leaked information (regarding the detention centers and the administration's hunger for their use) that he was genuinely not supposed to have leaked. First, to the *Times*, who was not interested. But they did know of a friend of a friend that might find a few hundred words of space for an article on the topic in a magazine the friend's friend published from home.

The friend, Jonah Jeffries, was interested, and told Myrol they could chat when he next happened into the New York Canine Hedonistic Retreat with their friend, Officer Hunky. Myrol, wanting to hurry back to Washington, had come and chatted with Jonah during his shift at the Retreat, the two standing in the big dog daycare room, talking above the barks and yips of the dogs, who did more to soil Myrol's expensive shoes than a year in D.C.

Jonah, minutes after he and Myrol parted ways, telephoned his sister, Tabitha, and told her of the creepy surveillance threat, which was perhaps more frightening in its detailed planning than its eventual execution, simply because anyone participating in a demonstration in the United States knew full well they would be photographed and documented by their representatives. This, perversely, was part of the point.

Jonah told Tabitha, with delicacy, that the choice of location was theirs, provided they chose the Bronx. Jerome & 241st Street, if they wanted the details.

The organizers, culled from all fifty states and several international groups, gathered in White Plains to discuss their options. Although they had not elected representatives, it was clear to everyone that without Tabitha, from upstate New York's United for Bitch and Justice, the protest wouldn't be anything more than John Brown's body hanging in Charles Town.

Tabitha related to everyone present the details she'd received from Jonah, who had been let to know that the Gentle Administration, were the anticipated 300,000 protestors to actually march down Broadway at the height of Tuesday's business hours - as they had been planning to do, beginning at 34th Street and ending in downtown's Battery Park - the administration would respond by flooding the demonstration with over 4,000 photographers. And these in addition to aerial photography by the two dozen helicopters, whose blades seemed to spin in slow motion when reflected from skyscrapers at midday.

Tabitha, characteristically, refused to consider relocating venues, and even threatened a sit-down protest, on Broadway, Tuesday *and* Wednesday, to stretch from Houston Street to Albany, thousands of protestors handcuffed in a line from one capital city to another. This threat via a long, persuasive message left on Mayor Gerdemann's Citizen's Redress Hotline voicemail: 212-UND-RESS. Tabitha was, Jonah had warned Myrol, ambitious.

All of this would have been extremely bothersome for the NYPD, Chief Jingo made clear to the Mayor, as his officers would have to perform the task of dismantling all of the protestor's cuffs, then re-

cuff everyone again with NYPD cuffs. And this in addition to ordering more cuffs from the supplier in the first place.

Finally, the point became moot when the Mayor contracted a large
mercenary horde of ex-policemen from New Jersey, the Varangian
Guard. The VG, in the three days before the scheduled demonstration, assisted the NYPD in arresting anyone on Broadway carrying a
sign in defiance of the Mayor's decree prohibiting the act, announced
four days previous.

This decree against signs made hard times for the poor bastards
who stood on sidewalks wearing advertisements for local businesses,
seven such examples being arrested two days before the march, all but
one released within hours, though five of these were eventually de-
ported.

The one held in police custody, Jose Jose Morales Alvarez, was uncle to our Marcenda Remedios Alvarez Johnson, and was missed at
dinnertime that evening in the Brooklyn apartment.

Jose had been, somewhat happily, in the midst of a mildly prof-
itable marijuana trade while standing on street corners for twelve
hour stretches. Jose, having been interrogated for over twenty-four
hours - by City, State and Fed - was all swollen eyes and miscellaneous
bruises and cuts when he appeared on network television at 6:45 that
evening, in footage never reaired by any network or affiliate, and extremely difficult to locate in more than crummy two-second clips on
webpages that never stayed posted for more than a few hours before
vanishing; seemingly no one having a copy of the footage, as though
the TV could take back what it had put forth.

Jose, who had never so much as won a game of *Sevenisima* in his
formative schooling years in Oaxaca City, appeared on network television with swollen eyes and lacerations, shoddily covered by make-
up people, to address The People. Rapidly, and in very poor English,
he confessed to selling drugs, and helping to organize the anti-gov-
ernment anarchist demonstration scheduled for the next day.

(Tabitha's widely distributed and little reported pre-protest press release noted that the threat, ultimately, was not to flood the demonstration with photographers, but with violence-makers, the *worst* thing that could happen for any sane organizer of demonstrations against mass violence. Her release was, customarily, ignored.)

Eventually, his eyes slit in fear (or to read the teleprompter), sweat standing out in dark splotches under the harsh TV lights, Jose even confessed to being King of Spain and the Grand Vizier, in a bizarre monologue rife with what sounded to viewers like painful throat-clearing. As uncharming as the rest, Jose eventually spit out, 'If you ass me, dee-moan-stray-shun iz berry good in da Bronx.' After which the screen went black and kind of burped a belt of static from its base, and every person in the US watching network television collectively held their breath for 1.5 seconds of dead air before a commercial for Coke Cola, already in progress, interrupted the dead air, and everyone breathed again.

Brock Myrol later learned, but didn't bother finding a writer to tell, that the entire thing (meaning more than just Jose's alienating, terrifying confession) had been staged, right down to the static burp and Coke commercial, *in medias res*. Mayor Gerdemann, that visionary, had suggested the tactic after realizing late one evening that the sensation of waking from awful dreams on the couch, covered in sweat and chip crumbs, could be immediately assuaged by a commercial for soft drinks. Plan A being that Jose recited the scripted monologue correctly and without deviation, Plan B had been to show Jose apologizing for the drugs and the demonstration, and then cutting to the Coke spot if Jose lost his nerve or flipped his shit or something.

(Everyone on staff at City Hall had been opposed to using an actor for the stunt. Stated reasons for the preference are impossible to ascertain, even after the invocation of the Freedom of Information Act.)

Mayor Gerdemann's Plan A, signed off on by anyone that mattered, had been to allow Jose Jose to mumble a while on air, until even the executives were embarrassed for him, and then move along to the evening's Sports report. This plan, A, was running as envisioned when Mayor Gerdemann's mother, Mrs. Evelyn Gerdemann, a not unpleasant woman no matter what one thought of her son, called her son to ask if the man on the television named Jose Jose had been hurt by her city's police force, her son's police force. Tell me it isn't so, my son the Mayor, my son Erasmus Gerdemann Archibald the IV.

Mayor Gerdemann assured his mother that, No, it definitely was not her or his or their police force that had harmed the man so, and could you hold a sec, Mom? The Mayor, his mother on hold, calling the emergency number at the IBC network and getting the Jose Jose monologue pulled and Plan B implemented in an impressive nine seconds.

Somehow, the mayor, his staff, and everyone at IBC had not foreseen the viewer's (as exemplified by Mother Gerdemann) overwhelming empathy for Jose Jose in its immediate reaction to seeing a man stuttering through obviously scripted English, bruised and paraded in front of them. This disparity between anticipated public reaction and actual public reaction prompted not a few research papers and articles on the personalities involved in the scandal (Gerdemann, his mother - not Myrol or President Gentle). None of these articles were appropriate material for the mainstream, though one did find its way into *The Beast*, a Buffalo, NY periodical as caustic as it was anonymous. The article, 'Jose Jose: The Man Who Moved Protests and Sold Coke Cola,' by Jonah Jeffries, quoted organizer Tabitha Jeffries on the not inconsequential fact that United for Bitch and Justice, after witnessing the Jose Jose monologue, did not wait to be contacted by the Mayor's office before relocating the demonstration to the Bronx, Tabitha admitting that no one wanted to leave the house, much less think about Jose Jose while marching down Broadway beneath camera lenses and helicopters.

7

Walking on solid but restless feet, over children and through caravans, beneath mailboxes and between old women. If Ms. Kurska, mine and Puffer's landlord, beat me to the bank and cashed the rent check had I sent her I would not only owe the bank the eight-hundred for the check; but the overdraft fee of thirty-five dollars. We had sent June's rent on the twelfth, which put it at Ms. Kurska's Long Island home the 14th. I had not checked my bank account online before leaving the apartment this morning - something about not spoiling the walk.

As with every month since we'd moved into the apartment on Morgan Avenue in August 2003, we had mailed rent checks so outlandishly larger than what our bank accounts had to offer that I imagined the teller not knowing to laugh or laugh harder. My only means of credit was bank overdraft fees. The bank would cash the check, or pay the debit transaction up to five-hundred dollars in the red before refusing any transaction - with the thirty-five dollar fee each time. Every month but one I had reached the five-hundred dollar limit; the one I barely hit one-hundred and sixty-five.

The sidewalks surrounding McGorlick Park were stained green with the pesticides that had run off from the freshly treated little lawns just inside the tall black-grated fence. Worrying about lawn chemicals while residing in Greenpoint was like a chimney-sweep fretting over third-hand smoke. We floated on oil here. Every neighbor had seen the neon green puddles; and smelled the flatulence of the spill, and of Newtown Creek, and of etc.

A child, seated in a stroller, looked at me as she ate small muffins, her mother gently pushing from behind. On our end of the sunshine, the sunshine was resplendent. East of Humboldt Street we were free, largely, of the consequences of rezoning: huge lots of property secreted behind tall, obtruding, oppressive slats of thick wood, painted blue. What were they so secretive about? Perhaps the scabs were hiding from Union Local 926? I tried to forgive myself for loving the neighborhood I was helping to alter; destroy? Those lots, soon to be expensive apartment buildings and condominiums, were for my successors - Christs to my John the Baptist.

Any store or business on Nassau Avenue that could get away with having open doors had opened them. Nassau, the busiest east/west avenue this close to the creek, was pleasantly populated with mothers, daughters, running boys; and stumbling men mumbling Polish. Within the Busy Bee grocery store, a young butcher boy heaved the silver meat slicer, gristle falling into the collection of rinds and scraps beneath. The store's open door was secured with yellow twine. The McGuinness Dental Clinic did not have open doors. Ali's Deli's door, across from the park, was held open by an enormous blanket, and an enormous Hound Dog upon in.

A middle-aged women sat in a lawn chair outside of the Nail Boutique, sunlight pouring over her. Her eyes closed and head slumped; pale and freckled. It was not unreasonable to think she may have passed.

'Why I called, Jonah,' Puffer said as way of greeting after I retrieved the phone from my pocket, 'is I just read in a Bronx local that there's a peace march up here today?' Puffer worked at a halfway house in the Boogie Down, as the kids used to call the borough.

'Surely, Puffer. Taby's protest.'

'Tabitha's? Are you attending?'

'Surely. You're not thinking of attending?'

'Yeah. I am. I am. And don't-'

'Call you Shirley, right.'

'Or Puffer.'

'Manfred, I'll see you there. 241st & Jerome. Noon.'

Puffer and I shared a six-room railroad style apartment. I was, currently, writing him a letter, though I had not set it down on paper. The epistle, prompted by a chance encounter with Puffer's old flame Vanessa Lai, was unfolding in my afternoon as I walked towards the train, around children and above dogs, flanking hydrants and exhaling on moving automobiles.

Dear Sir [began the letter], Considering your uncanny ability to briefly peruse my prose and tell me where it comes from - my history, and literature's - I should have just maybe thrown the baby out and kept the bath water. Which is to say, in my clumsy manner, that the second or even third draft of this letter - mentally - would have been sufficient, but a sixth? Well . . . . my time for ruminating is vast, while my time for typing is brief. But not to go on so, the purpose of this loquacious but enormously edited epistle is to relate that two nights ago I saw your old flame, Vanessa Lai, on First Avenue, across the street from Naked [Vanessa's former employer]. She was in a blue portajohn - one of those random ones you sometimes find on the street, as though left behind by a construction crew or being used for hidden camera gags for network television shows. Vanessa - and I don't mean to tell crude tales out of school, but the truth is the truth - had her pants and unders pushed down about her ankles (cankles?, you called them?) and was being X'd from behind by our old buddy Kayeef. *My* last sighting of Kayeef was perhaps five years ago, and he is none the less hairier (or scarier) for the wear(ier) (sorry, couldn't resist the rhyme once it showed itself). Anyway, he did not look like the sort of fellow who would be Xing with a stranger in a porta-john at midday, but I suppose the only one who fits that description in my mind is Karl. Although for all I know Vanessa and Kayeef have been Xing since time immemorial.

Vanessa [continued the letter] looked if not good at least better than when we last saw her. Her teeth evidenced a decline in amphetamine use. Likewise the eyes and hair. She even had flesh over the formerly harrowing rib bones. It did this heart good to see her in such fine shape, even if it were with Kayeef in a porta-john. (Please excuse my penmanship, Puffer, but while rotting away in this line for the commode in some coffee shop on Ninth Avenue, I thought I'd update you on the novella of our years, and its many scattered players, never to exclude Kayeef and Vanessa and the porta-john.)

Upon seeing that the porta-john was occupied [continued the letter] I said, 'Hey Vanessa!' and 'Kayeef! Careful now big fella!' before hurriedly setting off, mildly troubled and with a portentous quiver in the unsatisfied bladder.

Surf's up, Jonah. [Ending the letter.]

A tall young Polish woman with blonde hair and large blue eyes pushed a bicycle across Nassau Avenue, a hairclip pinched in her lip. Polish women in Greenpoint did have time for me, or for Derik, or for Karl. Or for anyone, as far as I could tell, who was not Polish and not from Greenpoint. The hairclip, I thought, is like a pencil, and she is concentrating very hard.

I glanced at some newspaper headlines, passing a newsstand. Were I in Palestine or Iraq or Afghanistan I would never have seen this lovely Polish woman pushing a bicycle across Nassau Avenue. But what would I have seen? And how?

A man with a heavy belly complimented a women's large fluffy dog. Her response was a falsetto exuberance in Polish. A nickel struck notes on the sidewalk behind me.

I knew that I had killed the Chihuahua when I felt the sidewalk against the sole of my shoe, though the Chihuahua was between.

*

The bug that was not dead had begun its ascent of the bathtub. Manfred Puffer watched it with patience and brotherhood. Manfred was pushing against the sink across from where he sat, for the abdominal strength it allowed him to project. He had been seated so long that were he to stand his buttocks and thighs would betray a toilet's ring, incomplete where his thin legs met.

Two water bugs also rested in the crevice where the bathroom tile met the tub. One is dead, he thought. I didn't kill him. Natural causes. They don't live more than a month anyway. If he had thought to wonder why he called them Water Bugs, he would have reasoned it was because they seemed so harmless. Conversely, if the bug were bothersome, or frightening - the cockroach, the centipede - he knew it by name.

Manfred had not planned to attend the day's demonstration, though Jonah had been gnawing an ear off about it for the last however long, in what Manfred assumed was some momentary, absurd proselytizing. Who ever heard of marching down Broadway? Or I guess it's Jerome now. He had not planned to spend the night in Washington Heights with Vashti, nor so long in her bathroom at mid-morning - so it was a day without preparation. His favorite.

When the bug crested the thick lip of the bath, Manfred rapidly tore a small swatch of tissue from the roll and plucked the fellow up. This was not the sort of bug to squirm or otherwise try to escape when caught. Instead it lay - or was held - docile between Manfred's thumb and forefinger, smothered in tissue.

The flush having finished its cycle, he stood to a hunch and looked down between his legs, finding satisfaction, the tissue and bug gone to seek their fortune with the rest of what had happened. I have my most elucidating, encouraging moments here. He was humming a song to himself to the tune of 'The Battle Hymn of the Republic,' rhyming Fallujah with Hallelujah.

The two officers in Vashti's kitchen were perhaps the most unsuccessful undercover officers in the CIA's hilarious history. It was their good fortune to happen upon Manfred, who attributed every noise in an otherwise deserted house to Pressler Dog, even when Pressler Dog was not there.

Harriet, tall and thin, bountiful red hair brimming beneath a serious brown cap, sneered at the sounds from down the hall in the bathroom.

'Do you think that's *her*?' she asked, pointing in the general direction of the sounds.

Her partner, Kayeef, very heavy and with more hair on his upper lip than on his head, thumbed through the copy of *No More Wacos* on the kitchen counter-top, rolling his eyes. He opened a cupboard and retrieved a glass, filling it from the tap and swallowing from it deeply.

'Who her?' he asked.

'Vashti,' Harriet hissed. Kayeef had not read the brief.

'Vashti. The bitch from payroll?'

'No!' She shuddered and froze, eyes wide, afraid she'd alerted whoever was in the bathroom to their presence. But the sounds emanating from the bathroom assured her this was not so.

'The bitch from Precinct 133?'

'No. The bitch-' She shook her head. 'The suspect whose house we are searching.' She paused, almost embarrassed for whoever was in the bathroom. 'Forget it, that cannot be a female.'

'You've never met my mother.'

Harriet's face was sour.

This was not their first visit to 459 156th Street, though it was the first time they hadn't brought drug-sniffing canines. As was customary, they planned to alert Vashti to the search in a few weeks time, whenever the paperwork got done, as was warranted by the PATRIOT Act. Or so they'd been told by their supervisor, who hadn't got his hands on the text yet either.

'I'd like to give *her* a Newtown Creek,' Kayeef said, leering at a photograph on the wall.

'That's her,' Harriet said.

'Vashti?'

Harriet nodded.

'Shit, I should've brought plastic sheets.'

'And plastic dolls.'

Kayeef did not pursue the conversation, though he wanted to very badly. As did Harriet, who let it go too. They had argued over the value of performing the Newtown Creek too many times to tell, always ending with he in favor and she in scornful disfavor.

'Who's there?' Manfred called, sounding like he knew he was alone. The officers smiled.

A printed copy of the Rig Veda was taped to a closet door in the bedroom, which was colorful with drapes and flowery bedspreads and the smell of perfume.

'Aha,' Kayeef said, mistaking the Rig Veda for the incendiary Magna Carta. 'And is it just me, or does it smell like grass?' He pantomimed smoking a joint.

'Ass. That's ass your smelling,' Harriet said, rummaging through the wide array of shoes and sneakers on the closet floor.

'These illegals are all ass,' Kayeef said, ruminating.

'And sass, Senor.' Harriet found Manfred's money clip - and its two-dollars and forty-cents - and mistook it for Vashti's secret underwear-drawer savings. 'And *nada* cash, Senor.'

*

That the Chihuahua's owner *was* Marcenda was not instantly apparent to me. 'How coincidental,' I thought as the young woman yelled in Spanish hysterics, 'I have killed a Chihuahua belonging to an Hispanic girl who does not speak English. Marcenda did not speak English *and* owned a Chihuahua. How strange, universe.'

I was transfixed by her reaction of high-stepping in place on the sidewalk outside of the green park; one hand over her open mouth, the other grasping tightly the Chihuahua's leash.

'No, no,' she said, alarmed at the realization that it was happening. 'No, no, ni, ni, ni.' Some of these sounds were deep, low reverberations; others were shrieks to pierce the sleeping.

I was surprised that no passing, or otherwise present, citizen paused to see what was transpiring. But a young Latina flipping her shit in the presence of her beau was nothing to raise any blinds about in these parts.

I looked down carefully, studying the dog's now-smooth features. 'Damn if it doesn't look like Bolivar. The hair, the skull, the baldness .... ears.' The girl continued to high-step in place, emitting sound. When she jerked the hand holding the leash, the dog's flattened neck and body would grossly rise, and then fall when the taut leash slackened.

'You fucking guy!' She was alive with vengeance. She looked like Marcenda. 'Fucking gringo!' She leapt at me, her long fingernails reaching for my eyes.

And a moment before her long fingernails tarnished my parent's gift of impeccable eyesight, we paused. We paused, the woman and I. I was bringing my hands up to push hers away from me, and I paused. We looked at each other with wonder, the woman and I, wonder and . . . . amusement? And, looking at each other, our bodies were lifted upwards, above the sidewalk and higher than the black fence running the park's perimeter. We floated, her and I, facing each other, perhaps fifteen feet above the ground, above even the tops of the highest trucks on Nassau Avenue. We bobbed in place, the girl and I, somehow centered, hovering.

The trees surrounding the park were in bloom. Branches scratched our heads and immature buds left white dusts in our hair. Row houses - three floors, six railroad-style rooms - behind the tree-tops all about us. The smell of sap.

'What you did my dog, Jonah?'

'Marcenda?'

'Si! Yes, man. Is me. Who you think it is?'

'Marcenda!' I was surprised. 'What are you doing in Greenpoint?'

'You kill my dog, gringo!'

'Is it really you?'

Marcenda looked down at Bolivar, his short yellow hair which she had rubbed tenderly between thumb and forefinger, over and over. All I could think to say was to tell her the story about the night he had sniffed my round posterior, in the midst of my cunning adoration of her, and then he had sneezed and hopped off the bed. And so I said nothing at all.

The child eating muffins and her mother passed Bolivar below us, their pace accelerating at the mother's recognition of the dog's condition. Some of the conversing old men, who daily talked Polish at the chess tables in the park, began to turn their attentions toward us. I waved and hollered, 'It's all right! It's good! Everything is good and okay here!' Thumbs up and smiles. Their postures and hard faces were unbelieving.

'Marcenda!' She was as beautiful as when we had parted, her dark eyebrows like black pepper over cinnamon skin. 'I haven't seen you in Greenpoint since-'

'You kill my dog, man!'

'-since, since what, two years ago?'

'Yeah, two years, when you run 'way from me on Greg's street.'

'I made a vow, Marcenda.' I had. 'I'm sorry. Man of my word.' I looked down. 'Sorry, too, about Bolivar.' I sighed, lying. 'He was a good dog.'

The vow had been made at the New York Canine Hedonistic Retreat, and involved money wagered by Colin and Derik versus money wagered by Jimmy and myself. It went: Were I to encounter Marcenda in Greenpoint - we drew a map to specify the boundaries of the bet - I was to stop immediately-

'No no,' Colin had corrected, his long arms waving in the air above the computers and print-outs, the cheeseburger in his fist dangerously splaying grease everywhere. 'First you have to affirm eye-contact. This bet is dead and void if no eye-contact is made at the start.'

'Right,' I had agreed, 'first eye-contact, then-'

'Then stop in your tracks,' he froze in place, not difficult as he was seated, 'open your mouth,' he opened his, 'widen your eyes,' he widened his, 'and raise your hands above your head, like this.'

Then I had started screaming (as the terms of the bet dictated) counted to five, turned with soldier's precision on my heel, straightened my back - still all according to Colin's dictates, approved by an agreeable Derik and Jimmy - and sprinted away from Marcenda, incoherent but purposeful, from Franklin Street to Provost: two blocks. 'Two, to be sure the performance is not hindered by a less than zealous cast!' Colin was, also, resolute.

'You kill my dog, man!'

I did not want to be insensitive, but we were floating above everyone's heads on a Tuesday morning. How long would we belabor this Bolivar business while not even on *terra firma?* I killed Bolivar. I did not want to declaim responsibility. But we were floating above Nassau Avenue on a Tuesday morning.

Two old men, muttering Polish, stiffly walked towards us from the chess tables. They looked up squinting, standing below us, shielding their eyes with open hands and using the trees' leaves and branches as barriers from the blades of sun. The shorter of the two bent over and studied the motionless Bolivar. He then stood, saying something to the taller man, who spoke to us.

'Who killed this rat and with what? And why is it leashed?'

'He is no rat, you!' Marcenda was offended. 'He is my dog and he kill him.' She pointed to me.

'What kind of dog was it?' the shorter asked.

'Lemme guess,' his cohort said. 'Chihuahua!'

I nodded as he slapped his thigh, cackling triumphantly, a mucousy sound in his throat.

'Can't believe it's a dog.'

'Believe it, brother.' I was short.

'You kill it?' Even with his height, he could not reach the soles of our feet. He hitched his belt and waistband with a thumb, removing a flask from his pants.

'Inadvertently. Inadvertent manslaughter, at worst. Like stepping on ants or- You know. Oops, it was under my foot what could I do?, you know?'

'Well, I wouldn't hang around up there all day, son, if I was you.' I nodded. 'They usually come through here one-thirty, two in the afternoon.'

By 'they' he meant the police, I later explained to Marcenda.

'No sir. Without a doubt. Surely.'

The two wove their way back to the chess tables, to explain to those left behind - who watched Marcenda and I floating as though it were being projected by some outrageously expensive and futuristic technology and they were not impressed - what the hell was going on on Nassau Avenue on a Tuesday morning.

*

Eventually Manfred's legs fell asleep. Cussing, he shook his head and sat up straight, closing the gossip magazine Vashti had left behind after a bath. Sitting up, his back cracked while blood rushed to his thighs, where for some time his elbows had rested, their points gradually becoming painful.

With consistent repetition he thought to masturbate, but did not. If he had no partner available, Manfred preferred pornography. It was too laborious to imagine all of the naked women – and so redundant when they were already there, somewhere in photographic form, waiting for him or someone very like him. And so he only let it rest on the toilet rim, useless and lazy to the world. There is time enough for everything, he thought as he hunched his shoulders and pushed against the sink, and everything takes time. . . .

'I spy a sissy perv,' Harriet said, reading from Manfred's journal, which she had found open on the bed. She read aloud the most recent entry, 'How Dan Rather Made Me Cry.' Kayeef tried to stifle his rasping laughter with a meaty hand. He was not afraid of being discovered. Rather, the idea delighted him. This was because he took immense pleasure in frightening women, and how was he to know that it was Manfred, not Vashti, behind that bathroom door, emitting sound?

'How did he make him cry?' Kayeef asked, bemused.

'Hrm, because because-' Harriet scanned the pages. 'News, one night, da da da, bla bla …. Here! "The unknowableness of why those men asked Dan Rather, 'What is the frequency, Kenneth? What is the frequency, Kenneth?' leaves me void of any assurances. Oh, the certainty of unknowableness!'

'Giant pussy.' It was a beat before Harriet realized Kayeef was insulting the journal, and not herself.

The officers were not looking for any specific item or information, but for anything general which could be used to deport an illegal. *No More Wacos* was incendiary but academic; pornography useful but only for the (in)famous. They wanted a weapon; a map with marks indicating targeted locations; fertilizer sitting next to a can of diesel fuel. Child pornography could be extremely useful, of course, however distasteful.

'Hell,' Kayeef said, spooning down leftover taco meat from the refrigerator, 'I'd take a picture of a nephew or little brother at this point.'

Had either officer known how easy deportation was in freedom's land, they might not have bothered with surveillance and just arrested the bitch at work or school. But, again, only Harriet had read the brief – and neither was up on Department of Homeland Security details.

The pressure in Manfred's belly had subsided with the appropriate effort expended. Yet he was cautious about calling the expedition off and buttoning up. There is something in the woods still, he thought. I must find it out.

*

'Do you still have the two double-beds taking up your whole bed-room?' I asked, swiveling in place by throwing my shoulders and waist in whichever direction I wished to turn, feeling no resistance – though firmly centered and stationary.

'I live Greg now.' I had forgotten her new beau.

'Good move. Great bed, I'm sure. Remember when we humped on his floor that one night?'

'Hey hey!' she called, her arms reaching out to me but not coming near, 'you have phone? Call Veterinarian!' Originally from Ecuador, Marcenda's English Vs became Bs: Beterinarian.

'Marcenda, why call a Bet, er a, a Vet? Bolivar is . . . . gone. Dead. Call a hearse or-' I stopped short of mentioning Greenpoint's impressive history of animal-carcass disposal – usually in the form of fertilizer.

'I want you call Bet!' Marcenda was beginning to panic a second time.

Passing beneath us on the sidewalk, I saw Darko, a local friend I had known since college. In the purest spirit of friendship, we allowed each other's lives to go on largely uninterrupted. I being busy with my wanderings; he with writing, publishing, printing and distributing his monthly magazine: *Bahai'llujah,* which celebrated the Bahai faith and sold relatively well given the limited resources of its progenitor.

'Darko!' I called, happy to see him.

'Jonah,' he said, looking up. 'Hey. What are you up to?'

I shrugged. 'This and that. How is *Bahai'llujah?*

'Excellent. Just confirmed yesterday that school boards in over one-hundred counties-'

'This is nationwide?'

'-right, nationwide, over one-hundred have banned *Bahai'llujah*. Banned it!' Darko was ecstatic. This, for him, meant a slight red grin on his otherwise chalk-white face.

To raise interest in the magazine – which was progressive or insane, depending on one's persuasion – Darko mailed monthly copies to Federal agencies like the NSA, FBI, CIA and others. This eventually placed *Bahai'llujah* on each agency's list of potential domestic troubles. (A *long* list, to be sure, though a complete copy of it was harder to secure than the PATRIOT Act.) This infamy drove up demand from the sorts of corners that read such samizdat, and Darko was prosperous, and busy.

He slapped at my shoe with a newspaper, missing it by far, saying, 'Hey, gotta run, Jonah. The Mrs. and all.'

I nodded, bidding him good day.

'What his name?' Marcenda asked, watching him walk away, Williamsburg and Manhattan beyond over his shoulders.

'Oh, Darko. Darkness. Whatever. Doesn't he look like the character from that movie *Donnie Darko*?'

She shrugged and pouted her thick lips, gesturing with her two smoking fingers. I removed a cigarette from my pack and held it up to her, filter out. She hovered before me, moist lips pursed, and accepted the cigarette. I lit it with one match. She pulled and the cigarette burned a bright warm cherry point. Her lips gently popped as they parted and she inhaled.

She stared at me through smoke; eyes red.

A crow landed near Bolivar, checking him out with little lurches of its head, like a boxer in a ring.

'Why you no jealous when I get wit Greg? You neber jealous.'

'Neber?'

'Nev-ver.' She thrust her lower lip from under her top front teeth to make the sound. 'Nev-ver. Nev-ver. I live my ex-boyfriend when you and me date, you no care. I dance with lotta guy at your friend's wedding, you no care. I date my best friend's boyfriend, you no care.'

I was confused. 'It doesn't matter much now, does it, Marcenda?'

'You no care. Now you kill my dog, you no care.'

'I keep an even keel, Marcenda. You threatened to kill and cut-up my ex-girlfriend, eat her, and feed her bones to your dog. I let it slide.'

'I neber say dat.' She stared at me, defiant, not having noticed the crow beginning to peck at Bolivar's eyes; nor the three squirrels on the bases of three separate trees, each eyeing the incapacitated prize.

'You said it and, I think, meant it. At least at the moment.'

'I neber.'

'You-'

'No, neber!'

A thin tear slipped from Marcenda's right eye and raced down her cheek, falling to the sidewalk. The cigarette's smoke hung about our heads, caught in the humidity. She had not broken contact with my eyes. I patiently – and hoped conspicuously – surveyed the scene below.

*

Though he did not yearn for public restrooms in the nostalgic way one longs for frequented diners or other familiar haunts, Manfred held a fondness – a familiarity tinged always with desperation (otherwise, why go in a public restroom?) – for them. The cracks in the ancient brown porcelain, beneath the black seats that did not encircle the entire bowl, were as comforting as a long retained cigarette lighter; or friend.

Of course, Manfred did not approve of the black rims' incomplete nature. Open at the crotch. For effective urination of standing males who couldn't be bothered with pushing up the seat? Or a prepared sanctuary for my junk when seated?, he wondered. But it hangs away, down, inward, away. . . .

He sometimes missed kicking the thin stick-handle flushers when he had not had occasion to do so for a spell. Or missed studying a stall's graffiti in the involved manner one was unable to when only urinating.

He sighed, thinking, I have my most elucidating, encouraging, optimistic moments in the bathroom.' This thought, when shared, had not amused Vashti; nor Victoria.

Swallowing cheese as though it did not need mastication, Kayeef turned to Harriet, who was still perusing the journal. 'I've got enough pictures,' he said, 'you have the mics?'

She patted her pocket without looking up from the journal, saying softly that she had the microphones which had been hidden in the phone and fax.

'Let's go already.' Kayeef was anxious. 'I want what she's having.' He pointed to the bathroom.

'Not on my shift.' Harriet was stern; and careful.

*

Beyond the tree limbs and cross Nassau Avenue, sounds of silverware striking dishware and coffee mugs settling onto counter-tops gave voice to Bea's diner. Though only two customers were visible through the storefront's ancient window, this did not mean they were Bea's only two diners. That one could see through the window at all was miraculous, given the two open grills beneath where potatoes and bacon and eggs simmered and scorched in pools of margarine. The window flipped up and in at its mid-point, allowing Bea to sell newspapers and coffees through it, when the weather was pleasant.

'Nothing at Bea's is over two dollars.' When I could think of nothing useful to say on a particular topic, I avoided it. 'Bea is sixty-four and she-' Marcenda was not listening. Her gaze, which seemed to see my most insecure depths, and to see through these depths, was discomforting. 'She came to the States from Greece. In 1960.' I was the one breaking our silences, and how I did not wish for them to return! 'I might've been jealous sometimes. On occasion. Of you, other boys. It's dangerous. Jealousy.'

Surveying below, I watched Bea approach us, negotiating slowly the thin pedestrian traffic on Nassau Avenue. Her white grease-stained apron, wrapped around her aging and thinning waist, billowed in the wind beneath her knees as she walked in short, staggered steps, carrying an old spatula.

'Hey, Bea. What are you doing over here? Ain't something gonna burn?' I smiled. Bea, looking up, did not smile back, which was her way of returning the smile.

'How you, ah?' she replied, speaking quickly with words slung together. Perhaps she asked 'How are you?', but if so the 'are' was inaudible. 'Is nice out today, ah.' Bea stated what was a question. I did not know if the 'ah' she ended each sentence with were a grunt, or a Greek affectation. Her skin, if ever tanned by her Grecian upbringing, was New York State sunless white. Her short hair, white and gray, was pulled back and knotted in a small ponytail.

'Yeah, Bea, real nice day. A beauty.'

'You want a coffee, ah? Milk, sugar?' Bea was direct, and diligent.

'Sure, Bea. I'd love one. Just milk.'

'And your friend, ah?' She motioned to Marcenda, who blushed and, with round and worried eyes, insinuated to me that she did not wish to have an exchange in broken English (Spanish) with a woman who also spoke broken English (Greek) while Bolivar lay as he lay.

'She's all set, Bea. Thanks.'

Bea shuffled back across Nassau, Marcenda and I watching. 'In forty-six years she's closed the place for fourteen-and-a-half days.' The thought struck me with wonder, and novelty.

'You tink we dead?' She pursed her lips again; I proffered another cigarette.

'No, I don't tink ah, think we're dead. Why? Because we're floating around up here?'

Yeah, man. We're floating here and. . . .' She pronounced floating as 'flouting.'

But what killed us? And what is dead? You think ah, you tink this is dead?'

'Yeah, man. Why no?' She was suddenly flippant; mild. 'Maybe this is dead. Maybe you kill my dog, then I kill you, then I kill me but don't 'member.'

'That's fucking ludicrous.'

'Why, man?'

'What about chatting with the chess guys over there?' I flung my hand out towards the chess tables, and felt as though I might be propelled into orbit; but was gently held to a center. 'And Darko? Bea?'

'Maybe dis is dead. Dey tink dey just run in you on da street. And don't know we are floating.' Flouting.

'That just . . . .' I was caught without words; how refute the abstract? The mystical?

'Is dat him?' Marcenda pointed to a figure over my shoulder.

'Darko, hey,' I said, following her finger.

Darko stopped beneath us. 'Jonah. Hey again.'

'You remember Marcenda.' The two exchanged smiles. 'Darkness, let me ask you something. Seriously.'

'Out with it.'

'Can you see us here right now?'

'Yes.'

'You can see that we are flouting up, ah, floating up here above you, above everything and the trees and all?'

'Yes.' He motioned for Marcenda to give him a cigarette. I dropped one to him and then the matchbook, which he employed and then tossed back up.

'What do you make of this, Darko?'

'I have no useful idea, Jonah. I'm not high or drunk. Crossed those two out on the way home.'

'Where are you headed, by the way? Home and off again so soon?' Darko worked strange hours.

'Yeah, I know. Rally in the Bronx.' He held up the stack of magazines he carried under his arm. 'Trying to make sales.'

'Oh, right. Right on. I'll be there, too.'

'Mm.' He thought a moment. 'So, I know *I'm* not dead, because if I were I'd of been dead this whole time, meaning all twenty-six years of my life. And if what I've been living for twenty-six years is Death and not Life, then I might as well keep calling it Life for all the difference the definitions would make by now.' I was intrigued and amused; Marcenda was lost but did not look upset about it. 'And so whatever realm this is, it is still one – since I'm sure this is the same world I was in yesterday – it's still a world in which people do not defy gravity like you two are doing up there and just float around whenever they like . . . or don't like.' He squinted and scratched his head. 'Are either of your dreaming?'

'Not me.' I had not often doubted my consciousness. 'Marcenda?'

'I neber dream dis way.'

'Neber?' Darko had no ideas. 'Well if it *is* one of you dreaming, and you have some control, dream me up some sales at this war rally.' He departed towards Humboldt Street, in the direction of the city and the looming cranes in the distance.

'It's a peace rally, Darko.'

'As you like it, Jonah.' He was walking out of earshot. I wanted to insult him with a prowess and class that did not sully itself with insults. Nothing came to mind, and he was gone, beyond open-door delis and salons and restaurants.

Marcenda smoked her fourth consecutive cigarette. She hardly broke her gaze from my eyes. The situation might have been amorous if there hadn't been a dead dog beneath us. Wind pushed and pulled her long dark hair over her cinnamon skin; and atop and about her head, tangling it into the branches. Her eyes betraying distress, but also hiding the indiscernible, unknowable.

'Your dog is being eaten.'

'Si.'

Her chin trembled. I recalled the sensation of kissing the small indented scar on her jaw line. But I am not looking for your love today.

Bea crossed Nassau, carrying a lidded cup of coffee in a foam cup. A kindly young man, obliging us both, tossed it up to me before running after his friends into the park. I thanked Bea and told her I'd be over later for dinner and to pay. She shuffled away, momentarily scaring off the crow at Bolivar's eyes.

'Fourteen-and-a-half days in forty-six years,' I repeated. 'In the early 90s, she went back to Greece for two weeks. And the day her son was married she was closed the first half of the day.'

'Bolivar,' Marcenda had told me years ago, when we dated, 'is de only ting I hab in dis country.' She pronounced country 'cone-tree.' To lose the dog was to lose, in large measure, contact with the last four years of her life. In the new world she had no family, few friends or acquaintances, few comrades at work, no immediate personal history with contactable others to prove that she, Marcenda, had existed since moving to the Bronx from Ecuador.

'I did not ask Bea to help us,' I later explained to Victoria, 'because she is an old woman who works too much and should not have to clean up a dog I killed just because I was levitating.'

It must have happened of a sudden, but so gently that it was not immediately discernible: we were floating back down to street-level; returning; slowly.

'I have to get to the bank,' I said. My head hung, staring at the sidewalk near Bolivar but not at Bolivar. My mind felt deflated but clear; downtrodden but realistic.

Once having broken eye-contact with me, Marcenda was never again to seek it. She looked about her: up, down, all sides. With what appeared to be wonder she looked up; straight up.

We were, finally, set down. A new center was found when my heels felt the sidewalk beneath them. I retrieved a foam plastic food container from a park trash bin and, Marcenda hollow and speaking a torrent of meaningless, unstoppable prayer, placed Bolivar within it. Happily the container had housed the largest of all chicken wing orders, and the Chihuahua was a fit; rat-tail and all.

*

Manfred paused, his hands doing the busy work of post-defecatory shirt-straightening and tucking, and placed them over his small but no longer youthfully obsolete belly. Sighing, he unbuttoned his slacks once again and sat down, with patience.

8

If I could have written a letter that afternoon – while maintaining mybalance – it would have been to the person who provided the majority of the body odor on the J train into Manhattan. My spirits were up, as I had earlier given a dollar to two musicians performing on the subway platform who were playing clarinet and bass guitar; caper music, but no danger there.

I, standing in the train, was staring at the city as we crossed the East River, above the automotive traffic on the Williamsburg Bridge. The train's tracks were several feet higher than the automobiles. I felt a kinship with those driving into the city and to work, though I was not doing either; and a longing and jealous loathing for those returning to Brooklyn, and rest.

Two girls across the aisle talked and laughed as one of them inserted her arm all the way inside a tube of chips they had been eating from to get the last bits. I formed and confirmed a personal judgment of the attractive woman sitting nearby, smiling and mooning over a used copy of *Lady Chatterley's Lover*. She laughs, I thought, not because it tickles her funny but because she wants someone (us?) to think she is sophisticated. I also considered whether she were reading at all. I was wicked.

I had helped Marcenda, who was somewhere on this train if not in this car, bury Bolivar near Newtown Creek, the dirt pliable and wet with the stink of petroleum. Then I had visited the bank. Part of the charm of my financial situation was that I would not know for five business days if I had beat Ms. Kurska, the landlord, with my deposit or not. Marcenda had, with seemingly nowhere to go and a heavy heart, followed me to the bank and then onto the J train. I had found her a seat and, slowly, inched away, hoping to be lost in the crowd.

The train moved lackadaisically over the bridge, as though afraid to tempt the supports with too much rattling about. In the center of a small wooden construction platform, below the automotive traffic, I saw a bouquet. Leora had, some months ago, seen a woman place the bouquet amidst the construction equipment, and then jump from the platform into the water. If anyone else in the city had seen it happen, Leora was not aware of it, including even the *Times.*

I didn't know where the person who was supplying the greater amount of body odor was sitting or standing. I casually directed my attention, in hopes of pinpointing obvious suspects, beyond the confines of the novel I held before my face. I wondered if in Dreamtime (heaven; the metaphysical) we wouldn't have body odor; or at least would be immune to it. I didn't think *Lady Chatterley's Lover* had been a very funny book, however desolate and lovely. In Dreamtime the past existed within the present. How would I ever lose weight, then?

I wondered if we'd all be homeless and starving in a world where the subway car did not have wall-to-wall advertisements.

With my nose behind my book, I could distinctly smelled the divine, unspeakable fragrance often worn by Marcenda. It was beneath the potent, organic and significant body odor. Was it Marcenda? Where was she? I loved whichever female was wearing the smell, and longed for her to see me.

If I had a second letter to write, it would have begun, 'Dear MTA, Please stop broadcasting announcements in the subway cars. I know, with certainty, that of the five announcements made since the J train came to a standstill on top of the Williamsburg Bridge, that nobody – the conductor included – understood a word of any of them. As sound pollution, they are akin to those fellow who walk around the city playing loud music on large stereos. In this case, in my unhappy analogy, the fellows are blasting ear-aching fuzz with intermittent squawks and squeals which we cannot cross the street to escape from,' and so on.

We're transferring to other trains, I thought as I did so at City Hall. We're walking onwards, limp and lame.

The handrail on the Uptown 6 train was hot from so many hands, the aisle crowded and nobody but those who'd been on since Canal Street sitting. I had happily pocketed the brief novel, *Walter, Waker, Bessie & Buddy*, before leaving the apartment that morning, and could barely hold it far enough away from my eyes to read, given the crowded train. A flash from the electrified third rail sent me into shivers. Between those installed by Lockheed Smartin and some other fellows, there were over four-thousand surveillance cameras in the New York City transit system. I shuddered at that thought, as well.

The most irritating consequence of the unintelligible announcements was how we all strained to hear them. Everyone hushed up a moment, and while recoiling from them, also strained towards them – the announcements – desperate to glean a word or phrase, fearful that this announcement could be the announcement that affected the way we traveled. I pondered my letter to the MTA and the commuting routines of MTA administrators, and if they themselves had ever attempted to *listen* to an announcement on the subway train.

Months later I received a letter, my address written in an elegant cursive, the envelope addressed to Senor Jonah Jeffries. It began, 'To gringo who bring the worst foul odor on the J train. . . .'

9

Everyone was wearing orange. Everyone, that is, who had assembled at

Union Square to participate in the protest was wearing orange. This in solidarity with particular inmates' jumpsuits. I had forgotten the fashion and worn black. Rubbernecks and the otherwise curious – police, reporters, photographers – wore the usual modicum of orange that persists in the American wardrobe: almost none.

I scanned the assembled through eyes squinting in the early afternoon sun. Manfred I expected at his usual hour: late. Darko I expected would be early, like myself. But perhaps he was still hauling ass down from the Bronx, after the 10:00am decision from Human Rights Our Us and United for Bitch and Justice to stage the demonstration in Manhattan, on Broadway, as previously planned and approved by the City. My mood, if any indicator of the general one, was tense; jaw chewing. Helicopters high above. How many? A thick wall of police officers surrounding the park and lining both sides of Broadway, stretching into the distance downtown. How many?

From the southern tip of the park, on 14th Street, emphatic voices issued from a small PA, hastily arranged upon an equally hurried stage. The majority of the voices spoke Spanish.

A group of students from Hunter College (one of CUNY's finest) sat on a railing nearby, having gathered in the park unaware of the day's activities. They watched, bored and bemused and mystified at what everyone was fussing about. Finding discarded protest posters, and their long cardboard handles, two of the students tore the posters away and played swords with the handles; posters become shields.

The park caretaker, in a red jumpsuit, glared at them minutes later as he retrieved sword and shield from the ground. The students did not notice.

One of the students, a young man with long yellow hair hanging over his eyes, noted a Wobblies group holding aloft the group's banner, which read: 'International Workers of the World,' a large 'IWW' on the top right.

'World War One?' the blonde boy guffawed, pointing out the banner to his classmates. 'That's over!' Happily, the Wobblies present were Hispanic and did not appear to understand him.

'New York,' Manfred greeted me, surveying the turn-out, 'ever and always mobile.' Through large tinted windows we watched shoppers in shoe stores and health food cafeterias. Healthy looking professionals on lunches; eating, talking, playing with cell phones; tourists and Moms browsing wares. They stared back at us through the tinted windows with unbelieving but confident eyes: Unbelieving that anyone genuinely cared enough about such impractical concerns that they would willingly waste an entire sunny afternoon on them; confident that the NYPD would clear away the rabble.

'Supposed to be marching by now.' Manfred showed me his watch. 'I show at three so I can leave by four. Hungry.'

'I doubt we'll match 'till four.'

At 5:30pm the assembled began the slow procession into and down Broadway. Manfred wanted to discuss ghost stories; I listened. Hawthorne, Poe, Lovecraft, Dickens, Christ. 'You and I are just one ghost story.'

'Not yet.' I was impatient and anxious, and did not see the relevance.

'We *are* the ghosts, Jonah. You, me, everyone here.' He motioned with sweeping arms to the marching assembled: predominantly Hispanic and, perhaps while still anti-war, extremely pro-immigration. Posters of pitiful, deprived Hispanic children began to appear and then dominate the demonstration's landscape. It was just as well with me. War on the domestic population – illegal or not – was as terrifying as war on a foreign population, in its own way. Fortunately, attacking the domestic population - Waco aside – did not mean military capabilities.

'Ghost stories fool us into thinking false thoughts.' I was adamant.

'Like?'

'They imply that one can come back – even in a haunted and spectral form. It is still a coming back. Human beings don't actually get to do that. In any way.'

'The communion of saints, the forgiveness of sins, the resurrection of the body-'

'Puffer-'

'Amen.'

'-don't-'

'Call me Puffer.'

'Or quote me the Apostle's Creed. I'm demonstrating against power.'

Walking slowly down the middle of Broadway we looked up at the surrounding spires. Here, in the middle of Broadway, I could see the top of each building, and through the windows to the people inside. People in casual slacks and dress shirts, ties, dresses. People watching us patiently marching down the middle of Broadway. How many?

Puffer commented that the demonstration being moved from Broadway to the Bronx was like going down on a female only to be told to massage her bunions. This was the consensus among United for Bitch and Justice as well. It was the consensus as well, we later learned, among the thirty-nine lovely fools who gathered together in front of the McDonald's in the Bronx that afternoon, waiting for everyone else.

A well-meaning but pedantic demonstrator ahead of us told her friend, 'We all have to be a part of the discussion if we're all going to be part of the solution.'

'But what discussion?' Manfred asked me, his voice raised for the benefit of the woman ahead. 'What solution? The solution to life itself? There is none. Only discussion, billions and trillions of discussions from all corners of the world, in shanties and mansions and boats and rice fields – what solution? How far away you are, Miss, from speaking to any of us.' Manfred was uncharacteristically imploring, though he did not speak directly to the woman – who did not hear him. 'How can life go on after you drop an atomic bomb on somebody? Napalm on somebody? After you destroy the cradle of civilization?'

'Yet it does.' I was steadfast; bored by the impractical consequences of the conversation; elated with the rebellion all about us. 'Here we are.'

'But so far from the center.' Manfred was, I suspected, idealistic.

'What center? Of what?'

'The world?'

'There is no center.'

'None?'

'No.' I was firm. 'I don't know. The sun? Consciousness? Being alive.'

'What about after life?'

'I can't cope with life, much less an after-life. Jesus, Puffer, stay focused.'

'Ah, Jonah. I *am* focused. Hayseeds go back to the country.'

Many of the procession's chants and slogans were in Spanish. We opted not to participate in them, though were goaded on by their good feeling.

The large policeman tore my shirt as he attempted to seize my body and carry it to one of the large police vans. Something had gone wrong. When something goes wrong at a demonstration, nobody is more frightened than the demonstrators, who came to walk a while, perhaps chant a melody, and then return home to warm meals and showers. What had gone wrong? Manfred stared at me as we stood in the middle of Broadway, his wide-eyes asking: What has gone wrong?

Glass broke. People shouted, screamed. It seemed easy to discern between the cry of a civilian and that of a police officer.

The large policeman, while apprehending a bewildered me, kicked the woman in front of me. I could not ascertain if this were intentional or not; or if I were resisting or not resisting the officer, who claimed that I was resisting in a loud and saliva-spattering voice.

A man collapsed in what appeared as an epileptic fit, though who could tell the difference with all of the flopping bodies everywhere?

Irritating sprays of gases threatened us in mists. I could not see Tabitha or anyone from United for Bitch and Justice. I was sure that Tabitha had not run away.

The large policeman tore the pocket from my shirt, spilling pen, tobacco, lighter. Instantly the rest of my shirt followed the pocket in the policeman's gloved hand, and I was carried from the middle of Broadway shirtless, my chest displaying my only tattoo: karl eats it.

I thought to tell the policeman that his hold around my neck was cutting off my breath, but remembered that that was the point.

Seeing spires above, I felt connected to villagers and peasants outside King David's or Alvaro Uribe's castle walls. We were a show of strength, sure, but only because we were a show of organization – which is to be feared. Carried from the street by a policeman, helicopters in slow motion reflected in skyscrapers, I felt I was being carried to Debtor's Prison; the Gulag; Guantanamo.

The National Guard (or whoever) was snatching just anybody off the street and cheesing it to NYPD vehicles with the abducted, as though treasure.

Manfred stood still, remembering his rights. It is unlawful, he recited aloud, for police to disperse people from a place they have a right to gather in.

They did not have a right – under the law – to gather on immensely busy avenues. Manfred shook his head, thinking he had seen our old buddy Kayeef, in uniform. I do, he told himself, I do see him. There he is, in uniform, arresting that old woman who had made the discussion / solution comment. What an ugly bastid. Kayeef.

Manfred smiled. I won't say I regret attending, he thought, but man oh man how I would love to be going down on my girl right now. Sour sweat bristles, hosh hosh hosh. It is unlawful to-. Disorderly conduct: The crime of being there. He imagined he and his protesting comrades – now fallen, hurried off, terrified, under control – attacking the police and helicopters and whatever else with hatchets, axes, garden tools. It is unlawful to-.

'I am less famous than anyone you know!' he shouted to the short officer who dragged him across Broadway towards a waiting car, door open. The people in the spires above still watched, coffees and photocopies in hand. I wondered if they had been photographed this morning as part of Operation Sentinel. 'I am nothing! I am nobody! I didn't even chant anything! No one has ever heard of me! Leave me alone!'

Manfred, crumpled in the backseat of the police car, wanted to say something heroic like, 'No doctor, just Jimmy Beam,' but his mouth being full of blood, he just vomited onto the floor.

I saw spit spatter from Tabitha's mouth as she screamed at a police officer who was arresting her friend. The vehicle containing Manfred drove quickly away. Tabitha disappeared after being tackled by an officer's huge flailing body. I was not wearing orange.

10

Ms. Tabitha Jeffries, while police officers and other personnel made gags (with both wit and rags; the witty predominantly about electric shocks and her caustically mentioned unmentionables), experienced brief but vivid and divine (she supposed) epiphanies. These she shared with the officers when she saw fit, as she knew enough about her rights that she did not have to say anything at all. The officers were well versed in her rights, too.

When asked, seated beneath fluorescent lights in a small room spinning with tie-wearing officers, how it felt to be an embarrassment to her family, race and nation, she proudly responded that she had enough shame to light up the city.

When asked, her heels warming under the influence of matches, Wasn't it ironic that someone as free as her used that freedom to infringe upon the freedom of others?, she wickedly responded that irony, in our time, had become a compliment; that one could state that something was ironic and that was enough to exemplify its goodness and value; that saying, 'That's so ironic' in response to a friend's told tale was akin to saying, 'That was an exemplary movie' when exiting a theater.

When asked, hooded and almost drowning, Aren't you committing suicide as you have no moral justification for withholding the information we are asking of you and thus, in choosing to withhold it, are choosing this treatment over a more graceful one?, she promptly responded that it would be a noble suicide, the first in the West since Tim McVeigh allowed the state of Oklahoma to do it for him.

When asked, tied nude to a cot with little in way of a mattress, Are you not humiliated to be nude and chained to this cot while an attractive man forcibly demands you to masturbate?, she devilishly responded that it was so pedestrian an event that she and her man called the act a Tuesday; and that there was just *something* about a boy in your bedroom.

When asked, her face aflame from many open-handed slaps, Do you not care if you ever see Bryant again?, she spryly responded that she was still young and could believe in love for some time and many hearts to come.

When asked, tied to a chair and surrounded by barking dogs, Are you not afraid of what it will be like to live on three hours sleep for the next however long you want to keep this up for, motherfucker?, she demurely responded that three hours of sleep, though insufficient, at least gave one something to enjoy when there was nothing else to enjoy.

When asked, after drinking an unidentified beverage and suffering the harrowing consequences of ingestion, How does that feel, little girl?, she cavalierly responded that her puking had been modest; and that vomiting was only as bad as heartbreak.

When asked, in the midst of several consecutive enemas, Where is it, cracker girl?, Where's the fucking nugget?, she energetically responded that they should wait, just a minute, it's coming, just wait a little, it'll come, I'm sure of it.

When asked, suspended from the ceiling in an uncomfortable position while dogs barked beneath her and extremely loud children's music pounded all objects, How you like these apples?, she wonderingly responded that she was having déjà vu; it was persistent, and intense; and that she would like nothing more than a tart Newtown Pippin.

When asked, tied to a pole while they danced around her, poorly mimicking Native American song, You gonna vote for Hillary?, You gonna vote for that cunt?, she cautiously responded that like the other

1% of the population, she thought she would cross her fingers with Howie Hawkins.

When asked, confronted with a flame and the notebook in which she had been scrawling the only copy of her only long work of fiction, Won't you be so heartbroken when nobody is able to read this work?, she sadly responded that yes, it was awful, the target market of a book was the literate.

When asked, her body splayed on the cement floor, face above a drain, Don't you want to save yourself?, she apologetically responded that she was not the center of the world; that there was no center; none?; the sun?; consciousness?; being alive.

When asked, the room's darkness bludgeoning and impenetrable, Aren't you afraid of the dark, little girl?, she ponderingly responded that weren't we afraid of the dark as infants as much as we were at seven or eight?; and if so were we all damaged from all of that terror we could not communicate?; articulate?; or is that another thing that we are taught?

When asked, as she lay in the room's furthest corner, Did you plan or participate in violence against the United States?, she humbly responded that the most violent thing she had ever participated in was a cup of Bea's coffee.

*

In the darkness, Tabitha wondered, What if pain became unavailable? But that doesn't happen, she reminded herself, anywhere. But I am in New York, she thought, hearing the noise of street traffic from a briefly opened door, unseen but not far from where she sat knitted into an unmerciful position on the cement floor. New York: ever and always mobile.

Alone with one officer, Tabitha asked, 'What did you want to be? Or *do* you want to be?'

'What is this,' he asked defensively, 'the Salt Pit?' Then hesitantly, he confessed, 'A sport radio DJ,' the man said. Then suspiciously, 'What's that look?'

'My expression did not change,' Tabitha said firmly.

'How do you know?'

'I'm trying not to laugh.'

When asked, her teeth being cleaned with exquisite detail by an amateur DDS, You like terrifying normal, everyday citizens?, she off-handedly responded that she was an American, and was proud to be the feared aggressor.

When asked, being removed from a sense deprivation chamber, How's that for being enveloped and obliterated by the void, mother-fucker?, she calmly responded that there was nothing more satisfying than a moment of reprieve and silence.

When asked, both cigarettes and cigars being extinguished on her calves, You want a smoke, girly?, she pompously responded that she would quote Oscar Wilde and say that a cigarette was the perfect type of perfect pleasure: it is exquisite and always leaves one unsatisfied.

When told, performing an act we won't even name, Where you're going next, little girl, isn't any country you've even heard of, nor their customs, she sanguinely responded that she would prefer Bowing's Jeppesen Dataphlan, and if they understood the custom of gin and tonic then she was not a'tall concerned.

When asked, her mouth held open and materials of an unknown nature being poured into her belly, How's it gonna feel to starve and have the runs simultaneously for the next however f'ing long we want, asshole?, she graciously responded that she was an American, after all, and that she ate on the run; and that she was always running.

When asked, her tongue alight from a pinch of pepper spray, Whatcha wanna tell us about United for Bitch and Cunt's position on the topic now?, she slyly responded that she preferred the missionary to all other positions.

When told, her eyes held open to watch footage of the demonstration while dogs used her legs and torso as fire hydrant, We know you know *that* person, and we know you know *that* person, and *that* person, and *that* person, she inquisitively responded that she would like to know if the media officer for the Department of Health would be available for questions and comments.

When asked, her breath taken from her with only one tiny punch, What you want written on your gravestone, chum?, she responded that directions to the nearest and finest eatery as well as the going rate of the establishment's *prix fixe* would be sufficient, as cemeteries were good for the appetite.

When asked, bent over a chair, her buttocks aflame with slaps from her own library, asphyxiating from the bonfire before her, You like George Eliot now?, You like senses and sensibilities now?, she glibly responded that manuscripts did not burn.

When asked, salt literally pouring into, onto and all around her cuts, bruises, etc., A bandage?, A bandage for a name?, You give a name and you get a bandage, hey?, she sagely responded that in youth one is desperate to cover one's wounds, but in maturity one is desperate to have them uncovered.

When told, juggling spheres of animal excrement while dressed in the robes of a geisha, We thought this would be funny, you can't even make this funny, she courageously responded that every jester knows the worst thing in the world is to be laughed at.

11

Perhaps because, after being thrown to the sidewalk by an officer, I already appeared unconscious, none of the police officers struck or kicked or abducted me as I walked from Broadway and the shining borough of Manhattan, dazed. Tall structures and millions of lights about me.

I smelled barbeque ribs, and imagined tasting them, which reminded me of Marcenda – and of years ago when we had feasted on ribs at an upstate roadside fair while I wished we had opted for Chinese or Thai. Somewhere they used chopsticks. Not that I enjoyed Asian cuisine particularly, but it would have been more difficult to imagine killing Marcenda's dog, Bolivar, with a chopstick through the eye or down the throat. Instead I had imagined stabbing him in the chest with one of the long blades at our place-settings; blades with edges so thin the food practically separated itself for fear. That was the sort of joke Marcenda would have laughed at but would not have found funny.

'Place-setting' is an admittedly grandiose term for what lay before us on the red picnic tables.

The tarp overhead was checkered red and white, and was meant for either a rainy or sunny day. It was affixed to a rectangular perimeter of roughly fifteen steel poles which were planted like trees into the soil. Roadside fairs in upstate New York were more austere than the hillbillies in *Texas Chainsaw Massacre*, but they were not exactly Madison Avenue, either. The chef, his belly hovering above the enormous grill at the far end of the tarp-covered lawn, wore an apron that read 'Smoke Out the Chef.' A picture of a chef smoking a joint and wear-

110

ing the very same 'Smoke Out the Chef' apron was emblazoned on the Chef's apron, and so on. It was similar to the cover of Pink Floyd's *Ummagumma* LP, which I had thought to mention to Marcenda, but knew she would only think the word was funny and repeat it, giggling. Ummagumma. Bueno.

Both Marcenda and I thought it strange that the extremely dangerous knives we'd been given with our meal tickets came with a plastic spork, cup and paper plate. No napkin. The chef, red-haired and thickly bearded, was not wearing a shirt under the apron.

Marcenda had 'been to da cone-tree' before, in Ecuador, but the whole thing got too convoluted to really say that she had been. Ecuador's capital, Quito, her home before moving to the U.S., was a robust and progressive city, about the size of Philadelphia. She had visited the country (that is, a rural place) in Ecuador, but while cities seemed to have just about everything in common the world over, small towns seemed better able to illustrate a country's mood and personality. I was really going on Marcenda's word for much of this idea, as she had been to small towns in both countries and I'd never been outside the northeast.

The chef did not have tongs, and so pierced the meat with the knife he'd been tending them with, and brought them to our table with a tobacco-colored smile. Marcenda was not hungry and always caused herself to vomit after meals anyway. She was telling me the stories of the New York Canine and Hedonistic Retreat employees; the illegals, at least. I did not know if it were cultural, but she called books and movies, as well as personal accounts, 'histories.

'And Camille come to the city,' she said, meaning New York, 'in 2004, with just husband and clothes.' She pronounced husband 'housband' and clothes 'clotes.' I smiled, recalling her attempt to tell me of the new sheets she'd bought me for a gift. 'New shits, baby?' I'd asked. 'Why'd you buy me new shits? I've enough of my own.' She had not laughed, and not even Colin bothered to make a joke about me being

'in the doghouse' over the sheet/shit altercation, as all canine refer-
ences soured irrevocably after six months of employ at the NYCHR.

I cut Marcenda's meat because she liked to be treated that way, and
it delayed the awkwardness of both of us cutting our own meat while
not being interested in the other.

'And Digna came from Ambatto,' she continued, stroking Bolivar's
head and gently squeezing his paws – 'pows' – his mouth opening in
a chasm of a yawn, like cartoon characters in toothbrush commercials
who can flip their heads open to brush the back teeth. The dog was
the 'only ting I have in dis conetree.' Was this why I hated him? Or
was it her limitless adoration of him? 'She come with her housband
and his friend, and they drive fourteen day straight, from Ecuador to
New York.'

I raised my eyebrows to suggest, 'Oh, that's a long trip, I didn't
think they even had roads the whole way from there to here, I wonder
if they had to take a ferry at any point,' and she brushed the sweat
from my forehead with her napkin. My only clean shirt billowed as
I leant forward to cut her meat, and I eyed my plate nervously. She
made a face seeing the pink meat, which she said 'Has mucho blode.'

'And Lejia come from Peru in 2003 with her Mommy and Daddy
and sister, on da plane.' What all of these characters had in common
was their continued illegality under U.S. immigration law; particularly illegal the work performed at the NYCHR. Marcenda, speaking
Spanish and being one of them (illegal), knew all of their stories and
where they'd been and how they got here. The most I knew about any
of them was the pronunciation of their given name; which I thought
effort enough.

For years Marcenda had lived in Greenpoint with her uncles,
Miguel and Jose Jose. The latter kept the family (four little ones, to
whom Marcenda may as well have been mother since Jose Jose's wife
had passed) alive financially by working days as a sign-holder in Midtown, advertising restaurants, shoe stores, jewelry shops. This street-
corner gig allowed him to supplement the laughable income with

marijuana sales. Enough to keep an apartment and a refrigerator with food in it. Miguel, meanwhile, among other trades, fished the East River at the Kent Street Pier, feeding the family daily on blue crab and bass. Sure, the Environmental Protection Agency recommended no more than two fish or crab per person per year from the River. But like the thirty-five percent of the Greenpoint and Williamsburg population who lived below the already hilarious poverty line, provisions came about by hook more than crook, though definitely the latter if bread or vegetables were desired.

I did not realize I was anywhere close to Brooklyn until I had crossed the bridge and set foot on Bedford Avenue. I smelled smoke but did not see it. I had told Marcenda she could stop by the apartment should she not remember the details of Bolivar's burial spot. I wondered where she had gone, and if she had exited the J train, or taken it all the way downtown and then back into Brooklyn again. She knows how to break a lock, I assured myself, hoping the apartment would be more of a haven from, than a target for, the Immigration and Customs Enforcement (ICE) officers, who were surely everywhere. The air, its industrial history be damned, was delicious and intoxicating, and I went about finding Manfred and a drink – if the two are not synonymous.

12

Without even the Lord's intervention, Darko and Puffer and I found ourselves haphazardly congregated at the closest (and only tolerable) bar nearest our Greenpoint apartments: Twisted. I wondered if the name originated in the bar's intention to be an LGBT hot spot, but did not ask the help. (It might offend?) And because there was hardly ever a patron, exclusively heterosexual or otherwise, it was difficult to gather the field information for a proper analysis.

Glowing Budweiser, Busch and Pabst signs hung behind the bar. Also dozens of bottles and cans of myriad varieties – none impressive. Four draughts. Christmas lights up in June. Two pool tables, three dart boards, one bartender. The floor, built of wooden planks, was oily and stank of a bar hundreds of years older.

I heard police sirens somewhere in the borough and quaked. We had left the catastrophe of the demonstration – the catastrophe of its aftermath, anyway – in Manhattan. But the growing cacophony of sirens and shouting outside the bar – plus the terrible and violent live coverage on the television above the dart boards – sobered my thinking dramatically. We need a plan, I thought. We cannot escape this. One cannot escape. No, one can't. They just keep coming after you. And coming after you. In the midst of this I wanted someone to love me, not solely because they wanted to, but because they had to; had no choice. In this way I could not be held responsible for the obligation to that love.

'A short story of my own.' Manfred emptied a pint so freshly tapped that the foam's shamrock floated atop the rapidly disappearing beverage until he finally swallowed it. He eyed Darko, making a dart-throwing motion with his free hand, to indicate that he would be included in the next game, after Darko, presumably, won our game. 'I just crossed, walking, the bridge.'

'The GW?' Darko feigned curiosity.

'To glory?' I was a whim.

Manfred defied us and persisted. 'I got piss on me.' He futzed with the crotch of his pants, trying to dry them. 'Pissed off of the bridge, underneath the walkway where the construction crew's gear is. Almost slipped on a bouquet some jackass left there. Almost fell over the ledge *inmedias res*. Is why the wet spot.'

'Did you say you pissed off of the bridge?' I was intrigued.

'Just a little bit.'

'Did you say you walked over the Williamsburg Bridge?' Darko faked astonishment.

'Mm.' A fresher pint was swallowed in the same manner as the previous. 'Car broke down outside Amy G's bar once I found my way out of that shit.' He motioned to the television, on which we saw that the NYPD was quickly closing down access points to all boroughs; fires raged somewhere in the city. 'On Clinton Street. Lucky spot to break down at least. Beat hell out of Victoria on the dart board and pool table.' Darko and I gave him the skeptical eye. 'Car sputtered all the way from 23rd and 9th.' His vehicular routes around the city made for circles, backtracks, unfathomable side-streets. 'It got *bad* on 14th Street. And worse with the goddamn dog in the backseat.' He sipped quickly a fresher pint. It was time for us to make a plan to get out of the city and we were not making one. To state that we needed to make a plan would have been so obvious as to be insulting. And without a plan to follow the statement that we need one, none of us could yet begin the discussion. 'Goddamn dog starts spinning in the back, as he does-'

'He spins?' Darko had never seen the spinning bowel movements of Pressler Dog.

'Like a washing machine,' Manfred confirmed.

'Or the blades of a helicopter.' I was not funny, as intended, however accurate.

'And he starts taking a shit-' Manfred continued.

''Humma,' Darko whinnied.

'Ah boy.' I rolled my eyes.

'-in the back seat of the car.' Manfred drank deeply a fresher pint. 'And it's fucking *hot* out-'

'Brutal,' Darko affirmed.

'The blazes.' I cringed.

'-and he's spinning and spinning and he jumps into the passenger seat , in the front, and does the bidness right there. *Right there.*' It occurred to me that Manfred might be running such a high tab in so short a time because he had no hopes of ever haunting Twisted again, things laying as they did. Being Tabby's brother, and his roommate, we would need to leave. But for where? 'And the car is shaking and dying in like rush hour traffic on the bridge and Pressler' s doing his thing beside me which then I have to try and pick up with a shopping bag before it stains and stinks the car up-'

'Did you say this was a *short* story?' Darko was precise.

'Were other commuters watching?' I imagined them horrified on the bridge; or at least amused.

'-and I just decide I've got to give it up and drive safely and take it, take the smell, so I turn off the AC-'

'Which doesn't work anyway.' Darko was correct.

'-and I roll down the window and the shit-bags and papers and other stuff – you've seen the car – fly out the window and into the East River,' Manfred's tab climbed, 'and I sputter off the highway and make it to Amy G's on Clinton before the car gives out totally and I block off traffic for five minutes, in the middle of the road, until some dude helps me push it into a parking spot.'

'Right outside Amy G's, huh?' Darko was surprised.

'And this is where you and Victoria meet every week anyway?' I asked a statement.

'And of course she's been there for like twenty minutes already and we start fighting-' Manfred was not interrupted but stopped speaking. He looked upwards to the ceiling and not because a pint was tipping back his head. He thought, I don't love her. Then, Oh yes you do. Only it's a different sort of love than the one you'd imagined. It's nasty, this love, and jealous and bitter. In chasing after her I have lost a part of myself that only she can restore.

'But clearly you can't tell someone what you think of them.' Manfred was stoic. 'Unless you love them.'

'And even then.' I pushed it.

'Yeah.'

Sirens outside. And on the television: Mass arrests, helicopter searchlights, statements from officials. They would track down so and so and whoever had done whatever it was.

Manfred watched me stare intently at the pool table's green surface. Darko watched the television, recalling the most recent publication of *Bahai'llujah.*

I watched Manfred's fresh pint disappear and remembered that being drunk gave relief and release from the other party, the always present, the everlasting. Meaning more than merely the State. Finishing the pint, he looked above the bar to another television broadcasting a football game. He liked the start of each play, how congruent it was, the merging each time, together.

Outside the bar on Driggs Avenue we poised our cigarettes for lighting. 'Bic-style lighters,' Darko said, performing the lighting ceremony, 'are really for marijuana. They're so transient.'

'But so are matches,' Puffer said, striking a howling flame for his second cigarette to Darko's first.

'But matches have history, class. They come from something. They're biodegradable.'

'And thus more transient than lighters.'

Darko lost. Manfred asked him what book was stuffed into his pocket. 'The autobiography of Gloria Steinham,' he replied, without offering Manfred a look at the paperback.

'You mean *Alice B. Toklas?*' Manfred knew his titles.

'Who?' Darko played dumb.

Manfred tried to clarify. 'You mean the Gertrude Stein book.'

'*Toklas?*' Darko corrected him.

'Yes. *The Autobiography of Alice B. Toklas.*' Manfred rattled out the official title.

'Yeah, that's the one,' Darko confirmed.

'That was Gertrude Stein.'

'Bullshit.'

I asked the Lord in silent, earnest wonder if I would know when I was dead. Darko's plaid suit jacket proffered the smell of dormant body odor in suit jackets kept in closets and worn biannually to summertime weddings. He had, he bragged, drummed up some impressive sales at the protest before it went to hell.

'The BPP tanks are on fire,' Darko said, scanning the horizon over Newtown Creek.

'And the Nashional Gryd site,' added Manfred.

'And the treatment plant.' I was not to be outdone. 'Hope it doesn't get to the Spill.'

'Well don't jinx it.' Manfred was frightened.

*

Manfred told stories, with ever fresher pints. He fixed the jammed quarter apparatus on the billiard table while telling a tale about beer, Victoria and coleslaw. Aiding a wounded dart, he talked about my sister Joelle, beer and himself. He called himself '*homo hablis*, the handy man,' in full recognition that he did not know what *homo hablis* meant. Darko made jokes, drank pints. The conversation gone heedlessly errant, I asked if we could stop talking about my sister's coleslaw.

Manfred stared at me as though it would spur my mind to think of a plan. I looked to the television, at the footage of the day's provocations and assaults by supposedly peaceful groups who had gathered without City consent.

'Wait,' Manfred whispered, hand on my shoulder, 'it's coming, just wait a little.'

Darko racked. Manfred broke, inhaled deeply, smirked, looked at his audience. 'So I'm taking a shit-' and he was off.

A quarter hour later, his toilet tale completed, he sighed. 'I should feel a lot more drunk for how drunk I feel.'

*

Darko left Twisted, weaving, alone. He was a publisher and unafraid. Manfred and I stepped outside into the warm night, breathing deeply Greenpoint's heavy summer toxins. 'You better thank your collective grandpas that I've got a plan,' he said. 'You should start writing this down. . . .'

13

'Something smells bad and it ain't the dog.' Puffer had compliments for Pressler Dog when we entered our third floor railroad apartment on Morgan Avenue. Pressler Dog was, characteristically, ecstatic to see us, and danced in circles in the hallway while Puffer hollered things unkind but which only added up to the fact that Pressler's after-work walk would be delayed while bags were packed. This did not quell his ecstasy in our return home, but greatly increased his anxiety that he would never see the outside world again.

What smelled bad - aside from Puffer's side of the place, all strewn clothes, old garbage, used dishes - was Greenpoint. Coming through the windows, left open for summer breezes, the smell of smoke was rich; not with earth, but the synthetic. We walked to the front of the apartment and looked towards the Creek. Flames jumped and blinked from over the rooftops. But how close? Queens? The BPP oil plant? The Creek?

We brought our heads in from the windows and lit cigarettes, our house-ban on them lifted for the day. I said something about being able to play beer pong in Manfred's room at any moment without fetching any glasses.

'Or beer,' he challenged.

The plan became a slow riot of packing what we could not forget, and leaving quietly. A few useful boxes scavenged from piles of garbage on the block served as suitcases. The unknown and unexpected congruency of things, I thought, objects falling neatly into meticulously detailed spaces. One of us had started music playing from a computer. Sounds echoing from empty shelves, abandoned walls, voices from the television, which was also on.

I called my mother, asked about Tabitha, who no one had seen or heard from since the demonstration had erupted into violence. The NYPD was not releasing information, and didn't even know yet themselves whom they were holding in the old Roosevelt Island prison.

Manfred and I felt brilliant in clean t-shirts and socks, undershorts. The smell of smoke was lurid and persistent. We checked out the window every few minutes, anxious to see if the Law was come.

'Surely we're on some list.'

'For what?' Manfred was frightened, but reasonable.

'We're on the organizer's list. Tabi put us on there, for protection.'

'From what?'

'Disorderly conduct.'

'And now?'

I shrugged. 'Who knew?'

I put old pizza in the oven, packed my bags and looked at Pressler Dog. Manfred entered and exited the bathroom, pacifying the most violent-sounding case of the runs I had ever witnessed.

Pressler Dog asked, How come all the packing, huh, Jonah? I said, We're leaving, Pressler Dog, we're leaving because they might come for us soon and do who knows what in all this commotion and so we have to run away.

Pressler Dog asked, What are we running from, Jonah? I said, The people who own the city, Pressler Dog, the people who own the state.

Pressler Dog stated, But we own the city, Jonah. We own the state. I said, Yes, yes, of course, Pressler Dog, and we'll all live forever on the city on a hill.

Pressler Dog reiterated, We own the world, Jonah. Not you and I, Jonah, but we: me and mine. You don't need to run, Jonah. We are safe right here.

We stared at each other for some moments. Often this meant he wanted food; other times it meant he wished to relieve himself.

Pressler Dog, I asked, what is it that you do the twenty-three-and-a-half hours per day that you are not voiding your bowels and bladder or eating? Pressler Dog said, That food you're cooking right now, Jonah, smells so good I'd better smoke a cigarette.

Manfred again entered and exited the bathroom, horrors between.

Pressler Dog said, Why don't you stay awhile, Jonah? Karl is bringing Anna Livia Plurabelle over at this very. I said, Moment? At this very moment, Pressler Dog?

Pressler Dog said, The five of us are going to HQ. There's smoke everywhere, Jonah. I said, I know, I smelled it. Five of us who, Pressler Dog? Manfred said he would go with you to HQ? What is HQ, Pressler Dog?

Manfred hollered - to be heard above the racket his *toilette* was making - that he'd better have a cigarette since the food out there smelled so good he felt like he had already ate it.

Pressler Dog wagged his tail. He said, Jonah, I don't mean to be alarmist, but my sources tell me Greenpoint is on fire. And talk about a fire that feeds itself. . . .

Who are these sources, Pressler Dog?

Pressler Dog whistled - or approximated a whistle with his thinly inadequate black lips.

Pressler Dog, don't you play coy with me. This is no time to be holding shit back, I'm about to flip my shit and-

Don't worry, Jonah, my sources know the ways that are clear, we'll make it to HQ-

HQ?! HQ of *what*?

Of United for Bitch and Justice, Jonah.

Tabi's group?

Sure. We're meeting there. With Tabi, Brock Myrol, the others. There's people to get out of detention centers; and of course further demonstrations.

I did not know if Pressler Dog knew what the hell he was talking about or not. But when facts are unavailable, it is only the history of a truth-teller that has validity, and Pressler Dog was a truth-teller.

I said, Pressler Dog, have you seen Marcenda? I saw her earlier . . . . Pressler Dog wagged his tail and said she had been and gone and no use waiting around for her she said she'd never come back and not to look for her ever amen.

'Of course, you can't trust a dog, let alone a Pressler Dog.' Puffer was resolute; convinced. And correct. We found a sleeping Marcenda in the filthy backseat of Puffer's 1991 VW Gulf.

'When we leabing?,' she asked. 'And does anyone smell smoke?'

Manfred, despite our proximity to it, had never seen the creek. What was there to see?

14

They dumped the bodies in the sea, from helicopters high above the Atlantic. This was documented almost immediately. Some of the bodies they dumped in the Creek itself, but as the *Times* had commented over a century before, the Creek's constant need of dredging made for an unsuitable burial ground. But there were bodies – some that would be missed, some not – from the demonstration that needed disposal, and taking a page from the Argentine junta, the sea served the purpose.

Newtown Creek was on fire. Five thousand barrels of oil on the BPP site had, quite accidentally, been set aflame when the neighboring Whiting Lumber-yard had caught fire, the result of strange, disquieting rocket fire from western Greenpoint.

The five thousand barrels had exploded, literally heaving fire all over the neighborhood. The Creek – which did not exactly need kindling for persuasion – was aglow instantaneously. An employee of BPP, Patrick Farley, had been hovering over a tank at the time of the eruption, inspecting. A hurtling piece of what might as well have been shrapnel had cut him in half, each piece tumbling into the burning oil and becoming energy. Jonah hoped Miguel had not yet begun his evening shift in the canoe.

Jonah and Manfred and Pressler Dog stood on Morgan Avenue, the BQE Expressway to their backs, watching the blocks they knew as home become silhouetted by the approaching blaze; and then becoming a small part of the inferno.

Manfred was on the phone with Victoria, who was in a taxi cab and telling him that all of Manhattan was closed. Nobody was coming or going. There were also some explosions happening on the East River, Brooklyn side, but she did not know of what.

The Thomas Percival, a Creek tugboat, exploded. Wood, metal, liquids sprayed onto the Queens and Brooklyn shores.

The plan, then, was to flee New York via Brooklyn, Queens, the Bronx – hugging the Atlantic until Connecticut and Massachusetts liberated the fleeing in all of New England's rural splendor. Victoria, fortunately, had been stuck on the Williamsburg Bridge when the city closed. At the checkpoint on the Brooklyn side she had given our Morgan Avenue address as her own, and her cab had been allowed to access the off-ramp into Williamsburg. The cab's driver, of course, did not appreciate being sentenced to Greenpoint – for whatever the duration of the citywide emergency – which was largely for the walking.

As there was also a checkpoint on the Kosciuszko Bridge, the plan was for the white female, Victoria, to drive over the bridge alone. Once in Queens, she would meet Manfred, Puffer and Pressler Dog at the Quanta Construction site. To reach Queens they were to, somehow, swim the Creek; inadvisable at any time, let alone when lit.

Jonah was only mildly surprised to find Marcenda asleep in Manfred's VW Gulf. That she had been able to gain entry without keys was impressive; particularly because Jonah and Manfred and Pressler Dog had escorted Victoria to the car, with the keys, just in case she should have trouble with the alarm. ('It won't summon the cops to Morgan,' Puffer said, 'but it may give you trouble at the checkpoint.') Marcenda had always been, however treacherously, resourceful. It was agreed that she would traverse the Creek with the boys, her cinnamon skin presumably suspicious to any anxious NYPDer at a checkpoint.

At the end of Apollo Street they climbed the brief and broken chain-link fence – really more a matter of stepping over than climbing. The heat from the Creek was intense, illuminating faces, hair, pores, nipples. The four peered up and down the Creek, but saw no safe point of entry. Fire owned the night, and had made it day.

'Upstate, we always called 'em cricks, not creeks,' Jonah said, shielding his eyes from the bright flames. His saying so did not, despite his intention, make their impending task any less imposing.

They walked southeast, to where the old Penny Bridge has disappeared. An enormous disc of fire flew over their heads and crashed into the Rushmore Paper Company. Marcenda screamed, though it went unheard under the cacophony of helicopters above, explosions all around, boats from the Fire Department and Coast Guard somehow floating on the fire, attempting to subdue it. From the old munitions grounds came the fireworks of rockets and echo of artillery fire. But directed towards where? At what? Or whom?

'I think they're aiming at Blackwell's Island!' Puffer shouted. 'That's where they said they'd hold demonstrators!' All four choked on smoke and flattened their bodies to the ground, sniffing at the dirt for fresh air. Pressler Dog was the most successful at both activities.

'Who is?' Jonah called back.

'Whoya think? *Them.*'

'It's all gone awry!' Pressler Dog said, panting. 'That's Brock and Anna Livia and the rest of us firing rockets, but they were supposed to fire them at Manhattan, *not Greenpoint!*'

'Why Manhattan, Pressler Dog?' Jonah was never too worried to be inquisitive.

'For the demonstration, Jonah! In celebration of marching Broadway! But now-'

Marcenda screamed as they watched a man throw first one small girl and then one small boy and then himself from the Kosciuszko Bridge. They were close enough to see that instead of landing in the water and then, if not expired, drowning, they landed on the dumping ground beneath the bridge.

'But now,' Pressler Dog continued, futzing with a black walkie-talkie similar to those at the New York Canine Hedonistic Retreat, 'but now they're just-' He broke off, shouting into the device, 'Brock! Brock!' A soft voice returned his calls. 'Anna Livia,' Pressler Dog shouted, 'the fireworks, the rockets, they're coming down on *Greenpoint! Greenpoint!*' He listened. 'Yes, yes, but this-' He listened, impatient. '*But this is not according to plan!*'

At the American Jute Factory, near the BPP, all of the windows shattered and scattered like dandelion spores. Or a star-burst. Greenpoint's and Williamsburg's power was out, but the fire illuminated the Creek and surrounding localities with fervor – as far as New Jersey, on the other side of Manhattan. Rockets from the old munitions site were now spraying south as well as north and east. Pressler Dog watched dismayed, devastated. The Haveymeyer Sugar Refining building near the Williamsburg Bridge flamed like an enormous bubble of lava, seething liquid.

The smoke and fire and general chaos and terror reminded Puffer of the paintings of Ralph Albert Blakelock. The view hazy, the opposite of crisp. But exquisite. Very beautiful. Discernible shapes and colors, objects. Romantic. Purposefully undefined – but, paradoxically, more knowable. A landscape so well known to the viewer that its most honest interpretation was the ambiguous.

Pressler Dog, ever clairvoyant, shook his head, sneezing. He watched the ghosts of General Howe and his large crimson army departing from the Creek at the Greenpoint Avenue Bridge, sailing west over and through the Fire Department and Coast Guard and flames, vanishing in the direction of Kip's Bay. Pressler Dog shrugged – if dogs can be said to have shoulders enough to shrug – and urinated on a discarded mayonnaise jar.

Due to the tide, the city's ancient fire-boats were kept from shore. At the end of Townsend Street, beneath the Kosciuszko, the Paper Company – easy prey – was gone before the Coast Guard could determine what the hell it was. Tufts of charred paper swirled, fluttered, burning brilliantly like millions of insane moths. Helicopter blades made the peaceful floating paper violent – and more gorgeous.

Jonah called to Manfred and Marcenda and Pressler Dog, who followed him without hearing whatever he had said. They sprinted beneath the Kosciuszko and along the Creek into the Keypan/Nashional Gryd Greenpoint Energy Center. Jonah's face immediately felt the radiative vibrations. Manfred looked up, waved to the helicopters. None of them had any good guess as to whether they had been – or could be – seen amidst the smoke and fire and shrapnel and debris. Marcenda thought she saw an Immigration and Customs Enforcement (ICE) transport boat on the Creek and shrieked, throwing herself to the rubbish-strewn ground. But it was only Patrolman Corcoran, rowing through flames, a helicopter's spotlight on him as he directed them with motions and inaudible shouting, none of which meant anything to the fleeing.

Jonah thought they might be able to swim to Mussel Island – near the English Kills and Maspeth Creek branches of Newtown Creek – cross the tiny lump of marsh, and swim the rest of the way to Queens, cutting their Creek exposure time considerably.

While the others prepared themselves, Pressler Dog happily launched himself into the Creek, mouth gaping teeth, eyes wide, tongue lolled. Instead of oil, sludge, goo – which was indeed soaking his heavy fur – he chased bluefish, crappies, striped bass. Reaching the triangular island at Creek's center, he shook furiously water and pollutants from himself before sniffing and digging at blue crabs – which fought back, to Pressler Dog's surprise and delight – and oysters, mussels. What Miguel called *Newtown Creek Paella*.

Manfred asked, not entirely rhetorically, if anyone else was wondering why Pressler Dog was attacking oil slicks and black beach sand in a playful fury?

A block of slum tenements on Anthony Street, aflame, collapsed. Dozens of Chinese and Mexican families immediately dead – although thanks to Greenpoint's Alderman McGuiness (who had raided the building the night before looking 'to give a coolie a lam in the puss,' presumably meaning a punch in the face) many of the families were safely jailed at Rikers. Due to the construction of a new condominium building across the street, the tenement's footing, unable to swallow the tremendous vibrations, had cracked the building months ago at its core in an irreparable way. The condo's developer later accused the tenement's footing of being too shallow for this busy part of the burgeoning city. Though by then the former tenements on Anthony Street were not big news, particularly on Anthony Street.

The Eberhard Faber pencil factory on Greenpoint Avenue plumed a delightful scent of smoke as it was consumed by fire. Nearby at the old munitions site, Anna Livia Plurabelle stood on her four legs and sniffed. Satisfied, tail wagging, she rubbed affectionately at her partner's calves. For his part, Brock Myrol gave his Anna Livia some warm affection before politely telling the NYPD Special Operations boys that they had better know exactly where these rockets were falling; and where not. The Special Ops boys, ever confident, did not bother telling Brock Myrol where advisors to the Mayor ranked on their Fuck You, Too list. Myrol, somewhat of an honest man for political affairs, was less aghast at the attacks on civilians and more aghast at the attacks on industry. But Mayor Gerdemann ran a complex administration.

The water in the Creek was tepid and not blazing near Mussel Island. Jonah congratulated himself for his insightful planning and told Marcenda she would probably want to be topless while swimming the Creek. She slapped him and dove into the water, he and Manfred following. All three employed the breast stroke. All three vomited en route. Pressler Dog was already waiting on the swampy island shore, bushy tail wagging vigorously. Looking towards the Queens neighborhood of Maspeth, Pressler Dog saw the Reverend John Doughty and a large gathering of Puritans attacking some Mespat Indians on the shore of the Creek. The Indians fought back, and were victorious. Pressler Dog stared curiously skyward as the spirits of the Puritans and Indians ascended, forming new spirits as they left. For a moment the land was chestnut trees, birch, conifers. Then fire, again.

They reached the island and emerged from the Creek shivering, vomiting, tired. A barge named the Minerva B carrying eight hundred tons of coal sank without making a discernible sound.

Jonah mentioned that Greenpoint was once pronounced 'Green pernt' and, giddy that they had made it as far as they had, pinched Marcenda, then jumped, performing an elaborate entrechat.

*

Were there any luck in having to traverse the lit creek, it was that Jonah and Manfred and Marcenda, not to mention a sensitive Pressler Dog, did not have to witness the various unflattering public displays that occurred throughout Greenpoint and Williamsburg as the neighborhoods exploded and, through the fist of the City and even the Feds, were locked down. An angry population, terrified and ignorant of what was happening around them, huddled in their homes when possible. When not, they sought seclusion in whatever restaurant or warehouse or condominium offered easiest access. Sometimes, though not often, windows were broken, doors unhinged and even individuals beaten for this purpose. But the general violence of law enforcement bodies trying to secure the area, as well as the wildly inconsistent rockets, largely made such vandalism unnecessary.

The various local papers, and the *Times*, were immediately very busy writing of the events, though as usual the television cameras beat them to the earliest coverage, if not the most contextualized. Only the major networks were allowed access over Brooklyn's rooftops as the city, for the moment, became a no-fly zone, resulting in much the same air traffic as Baghdad, noted one well-traveled journalist.

Manfred was readying Pressler Dog for the rest of the creek voyage by removing as many clinging crabs and clams from the dog's body as was possible, given the sticky circumstances. Jonah, perhaps only because he was friendly, was making passes at the tall and blonde Tin Can Mary, who, with her father, was the only inhabitant of Mussel

Island. Their homestead, a series of shacks and various smelting and cooking apparatuses, was known as Tin Can Point. It was here that Mary's father, called The Fellow (as in, The Fellow from Tin Can Point), brought together the tin cans and various tin objects he'd scavenged from around the neighborhood and melted everything to liquid, for solder.

Marcenda knocked over some cooking equipment and was scolded by The Fellow, who cursed through his thick and grotesquely overgrown beard. Pressler Dog made the mistake of referring to Mary as Tin Can Mary, and Manfred made the mistake of laughing, and she threw some hunks of very hot tin at them, barely missing. The tin sizzled in the creek, sinking. For all of their isolation and strangeness, Mary and father were shocked to disbelief that we had just swum the creek, let alone were about to do it again. The Fellow said he would offer his canoe, but wouldn't. Jonah scrawled his number on a slip of paper for Mary, who threw it into a smelter.

It was not long before the Grand Street, the Kosciuszko, and the Greenpoint Avenue bridges were aflame. Due to the checkpoints, traffic was somewhat easily maneuvered off of the bridges and into the neighborhoods, where distraught and frightened drivers abandoned their cars, made frustrated cell phone calls which did not connect, and risked it on foot through Brooklyn.

At the Greenpoint Oil Terminal alongside Whale Creek, firemen sprayed water all over the oil tanks, in the hopes of keeping them cool enough that they resisted the immense heat emanating from the flames not only on the creek but consuming the Harco Chemical and Diamond Asphalt locations nearby, which were enormously lit.

Jonah and Pressler Dog waved to Patrolman Corcoran as he passed Mussel Island in his canoe, guiding an enormous Fire Department boat, itself towing a burning barge towards the East River. The Department had tugged over a dozen burning crafts that way thus far, though the ships and boats and barges only drifted towards Blackwell

Island, which was not itself burning as yet, though was entirely surrounded by flaming ships and cargo.

An errant and flaming hunk of wind flew overhead and everyone but The Fellow ducked. All around them meteorites of paper, wood, oil and garbage spread the fire. On the Queens side of the creek, where Victoria waited, the Dry Ice Corporation and the Phelps Bodge plants sizzled, waiting to erupt.

At the site of the old Penny Bridge, where the Coast Guard had first spotted evidence of what was now known as the Greenpoint Oil Spill, Jonah watched, frenzied but helpless, as flaming objects of he did not know what came from somewhere and struck the Immobile Oil facility, the base of clean-up operations.

Allowing his imagination to run wild - and why not? - Jonah envisioned the fire devouring the facility and setting aflame not only the equipment beneath, but the oil it was purportedly removing from beneath the neighborhood. All 30 million gallons. Jonah wanted a cigarette so devoutly he tried to light the wet ones from his pocket, which did not take to flame. He thought of Centralia, Pennsylvania; and the gross relief of surrender.

Despite the NYFD's best efforts, the tanks at the Greenpoint Oil Terminal exploded, heaving flaming oil up, down and everywhere else. Cries of human suffering were prevalent, however deafened.

An anonymous party was sure to take the opportunity to deface the bust of Solidarity priest Rev. Jerzy Popieluszko on Driggs Avenue for the second time in its history.

Jonah and Marcenda stood on Creek's edge, eyeing Queens, preparing for the swim, waiting for Manfred and Pressler to finish urinating. A short man approached them, unwrapped something from a newspaper - a human head, black water - and looked up at them helplessly. Jonah took the Lord's name in vain; Marcenda threw stones at the man until he ran off, hurling the head into the creek.

Pressler Dog saw familiar Mespat Indians rowing past the Island. They nodded stoically to him as they lapped the East River Kayak Club, who were justly embarrassed.

All parties stopped, the fire a background momentarily, to watch a policeman lasso a calf who was floating in the creek, having escaped a nearby slaughterhouse. This policeman also found that night in the creek a body tied to an iron rod, six feet in length, which ran the body's backside; the body and iron encased in burlap. Both findings were trivial on such an evening, certainly, however altering for the policeman.

Pressler Dog was, again, the most eager to take on the waves. He leapt with glee, and a running start, into the flaming water, tongue lolling, eyes brilliant balls of anticipation.

Jonah and Marcenda and Manfred snuck into the water, beneath the surface. Jonah asked, What's the difference when we gotta come up for air in this shit anyway? Manfred answered, We're swimming this whole fucking thing in one breath, hayseed, asthma or no. We'd better hope to our collective grandpas that there's a reason this is called a creek and not a river, Jonah said.

Did I mention, Pressler hollered back to Jonah, that I'm pretty serious with a doggy paddle? Pressler Dog did not wait for a response to resume his quick career of the creek. He whistled a tune, chuckled, and was about to call back something about his wagging tail being the finish line, suckas, when he froze in place, for fear, and slowly began sinking.

Above Pressler's head appeared the enormous apparition of Wooden Leg Stuyvesant, former Governor of New Amsterdam. His large nose extended so far that it seemed to point accusingly at Pressler, who whined softly. A wart sat atop the nose's tip. Stuyvesant held a brown weathered cane that came to a sharp point; and wore only a nightgown, which flapped loosely about his bony, opaque frame. He sang,

'My witty, pretty Pressler pup,
I've come to take you for my 'sup.
Your tales are wicked, but are not lies,
Your tale isn't wagging, I'll have it fried.'

Stuyvesant went on in this manner for some time, a horror-stricken Pressler Dog sinking slowly beneath the surface of the water, unable to move. The sixth or seventh verse went,

'And Pressler Dog, don't you think I know
Of all your plans to take my soul
With witch's brew from Tin Can Point
And something called a Greenpernt Joint?'

And generally the same paranoid motifs for another few verses which, however truthful, were outlandishly difficult for anyone to comprehend in all the madness, let alone a Pressler Dog, who sank and sank and sank, a puppy stone.

Happily, a passing Manfred, oblivious of the Governor above the surface, caught an impossibly hairy object he immediately recognized as his Pressler Dog and, tucking the dead weight under his arm, swam more fiercely to the Queen's edge, and a new breath.

15

'This moon's gonna rise tonight, and rise holy.' Puffer, his elbow bent and arm on the window ledge, was prophetic as he drove the vehicle through the evening. 'This I promise thee, children of New York – and wherever it is you're from, Marcenda.' He improvised a long-winded but amusing prayer, reverently closing, 'So I'm ordering up a moon here, God. That's one big, well hung moon over Falcon Ridge. Nine-ish. *Mea culpa terra firma gatito.*'

As we fled north, the train that sallied beside and past our white, cramped and immortal VW Gulf sounded like a harmonica heard through a wall. Victoria sat passenger seat, wearing sunglasses and trying every conceivable maneuver to avoid being directly struck by the late-setting sun. She spoke rapidly and excitedly with Marcenda, who sat beside me in the backseat, and who was also fleeing. Women together: let me hear and greet your comment with a laugh of understanding. I have a mother, too. I have or have had heartaches, too. Our lives are so similar; how important and interesting yours is to me, and mine to you.

Pressler Dog was wiped out from all of the adventures, and slept soundly on the floor at our feet, his long body splayed across the width of the VW.

'I can't wait to wake in a tent with you and Puffer in the wilderness.' Victoria grabbed my ear and yanked, playfully. Then, smiling, said to Marcenda, 'You've seen the wallet-sized picture of Puffer in their bathroom?'

Marcenda had. She nodded. 'Every morning when 'dis guy,' she snookered my side, 'when he shave-' She stopped, laughing, scratching at my week's worth of messy beard, and correcting herself said, 'Every morning when he get his toothbrush-' She stopped again. Victoria's and Manfred's laughter joined Marcenda's in chorus. She tried again. 'In da morning when he comb-' Even I chuckled. Marcenda finished, 'Every morning when Jonah need pee, he passes picture of Puffer. *Super dulce.*'

I translated for Victoria and Puffer: 'Very sweet.'

I told Marcenda that combing my hair was about as foreign to me as douching.

When the rain began somewhere near White Plains, the squeak of the windshield wipers sounded like children laughing.

*

The squeak of the windshield wipers sounded like children laughing. Victoria had assumed the wheel, as Manfred had been imbibing. The night was dark, with few lights – residential, business, street – illuminating the roadway as we drove through forest. An inexplicable myriad of frogs jumped from the ditch into traffic in heedless efforts to cross the curiously busy rural road. I watched, miles unending, their long legs extend behind their airborne bodies. The splayed, web-footed silhouettes against the headlight-lit brush of the roadside.

Marcenda and Manfred slept in the backseat, flush with alcohol, murmuring dreams. Her mouth sensuous with spittle on her lips; his dry and snoring.

Victoria being the driver, it was left to me to be loquacious. I was, fortunately for the task at hand, mildly inebriated; though conscious enough not to mention the frogs, fearing her horror. How she accounted for the thudding on the automobile as the bodies bounced and thwacked on all sides and tops and bottoms was her affair.

I was in the process of responding to her query, What did you talk to Pastor Dan about for so long at Puffer's sister's wedding, so many moons ago?

'Well Pastor Dan,' I said, 'I've known Pastor Dan since-. Well he's always been this peripheral figure in the midst of my mist, this morass of-. So for like fifteen years I've known this guy though I've spent less time with him in those fifteen years than I have with you in what ..... six months?' I affectionately removed my hand from my crotch to pinch her knee. 'See Pastor Dan wasn't my pastor but Manfred's, who I knew through Kayeef. And Pastor Dan is always, I think, eager to pick my brain a little since he knows my dad is a preacher and that I'm not much into Jesus anymore and I think he likes to-. He likes to hear what the diners have to say about the restaurant. And this is a chain operation.'

Marcenda was to depart some time after she woke. She did not know where because she did not have a why. Why this place and not that one? The only place for her to go was right back to New York, starting a different life, with different haunts and different commutes and places of employment.

'So I find it interesting to hear what a Christian who I'm not related to has to say about lots of questions I'd like to ask Christians but can't ask people I'm related to. Because I don't like to ask questions of my mom that prompt her to imagine me burning in eternal damnation, the broken teeth, screaming. And doing your laundry is so expensive.'

'In hell.' She played along, stating the question flatly.

'Right. It's good to make jokes about hell. Because it's right here.' I made a sweeping gesture with my hand to show that I meant life, existence, the world. 'And but in turn Pastor Dan gets to hear the opinion of a person who knows – or used to know – his B-I-B-L-E but does not deem it an authority. Sometimes the analogy I make is that a warden interviews an escaped prisoner to learn how and why the fellow escaped. The why being obvious, right?' Flashes of wet leaves and trees when an oncoming car illuminated the forest. 'And so we just chatted about the war – well, both of them; all of them? – and health care and citizen's responsibility and he went on about Islamo

Fascism which I just couldn't *not* roll my eyes and smirk about even though I know it's dick to do so. Because if you're an outside observer of the whole thing, who has killed more of who? Us? Or Islamo Fascists?' I kept saying 'because' as though she had asked repeated questions, though she had not.

The driver in front of us applied the brake incessantly – the red light shining on our faces through the windshield – while traveling 55mph on a rural road. Victoria liked hearing someone talk, even if she was not listening. My voice was far less assuming and hungry than AM radio. His touching his crotch and then my knee, she thought, it's a trusting gesture.

My breath had been overpoweringly odoriferous, due to Guinness, until I'd started smoking and the windows went down. The mist outside was no longer rain.

She opened her mouth to change the subject, but did not want to interrupt me, and didn't. Then maybe he'd never get started again, she thought. I know how he is. Sulk if you interrupt him as though it means you don't give a shit about anything he has ever or will ever say. She had conversed with Pastor Dan and I at the table on the deck overlooking Lake Ontario for the last hour of Manfred's sister's reception. Two years ago? She participated when something of interest was said, and otherwise watched over the large still water. How can he stand to go on and on like that with Pastor Dan about all that Christianity? I like discussing my past, too, but it usually involves *me*, not just ideas ideas ideas.

Thwack thwack thwack. I hope he doesn't hear me killing all these frogs. He's so sensitive. Probably say some internal prayer, imagining all the frog souls – which he doesn't even believe in! – floating into the ether. He believes in that though! Ether! Well, I believe in gravity. I just wish this fuckstick would stop breaking every goddamn twenty-. Seconds. God I hope Manfred's not so fucked up he-. What? She swatted down the turn signal and passed the car in front of us, racing along the dotted yellow lines, then flicking the signal back up to assume the correct lane. That cake was too big. I don't like ostentation. The dancing was fun.

Marcenda did not want to venture into New England, and she left us for a bus stop in the Berkshires, unsure of what bus would come and when, let alone where it was going. She thanked me for the ride, her fingers on my bearded cheek, then slapped me for killing Bolivar. And insisted we leave, da bus will come, you, da bus will be berry berry quick in come to take me good places!, she smiled and flung her hands into the air, merrily.

Thwack.

16

Everyone had a poncho but me. Rain was predicted for the first night of the 2006 Falcon Ridge Folk Festival, and all we would have on the muddy hillside as deterrent was the blue tarp we'd been sitting on since arriving from New York – and the ponchos. The tarp – muddy, grass-covered, full of holes – at least largely kept us from bugs and damp earth.

The sun was pondering setting but had not yet decided to do so. Julie Jacklet, who still lived in the upstate region Manfred and I had fled, was due to the festival anytime. The heat gave the afternoon an anxiousness, made the grass thicker and the people more mysterious. But the heat was fading; if not the mystery.

Victoria persuaded me into perusing the Dance Tent while Manfred visited the portable toilets. She talked me into dancing, too, which we did with an old couple who knew their steps and soon tired of our embarrassing gyrations and kicks. My friend's girlfriends were always very nice to me. I gathered it was because I never tried to sleep with them.

'We are amidst the cornfields and baseball diamonds,' I said, feeling pastoral, belching the greasy diner breakfast eaten that morning before ponchos has been purchased by all but me. They were only four dollars, but if the rain held off I'd have felt swindled. I wouldn't wear one anyway. Victoria was wearing a horizontally-striped black and white shirt and, in tandem with the yellow poncho, took on the semblance of a honey bee. 'The cutest damned thing I've ever seen,' Manfred said, dumping ice into a cooler. For a moment I thought I saw an enormous ice cube on the ground, until I recognized the tax stamp and saw it was discarded cellophane from a cigarette pack.

The Falcon Ridge Folk Festival was staged every July in Hillsdale, New York, 90 miles north of the city. We were planning to visit Alice's Restaurant (very close by), as well as the Eastern Correctional Facility gift shop on Saturday. Victoria and I did not particularly enjoy folk music, 'Be it anti-folk,' she said, wiping the grease from the day's last fried dough onto her pants, the moon hung low over yonder mountain ridge as we had requested it, 'new-folk, old-folk, agit-folk-'

'Fuck folk.'

'I haven't heard that one.'

Each act on the main stage gave way to the next throughout the afternoon and evening. We lay on the lawn, fetching beverages and meals from the town of tented vendors west of the main stage, and by evening everyone but Puffer was feeling chatty. He had stumbled off to take a nap in the high weeds, away from the crowded lawn nearer the stage. 'I'd like to be able to smoke,' he had said in explanation, 'when and if I wake, now and then.' Julie, arrived from Syracuse, had found some friends from yesteryear and was somewhere up high on the hill, opposite Manfred. Victoria joked that Manfred would, without waking, come tumbling down from the peak of the hillside, roll downhill through the assembled audience and right up onto the stage – but have nothing to sing.

'I hope whoever Julie Jacklet marries doesn't force her to change her name,' I said.

Victoria looked at me quizzically before nodding and fussing with her hair, which lay all about her in the grass. A mosquito buzzed in my ear and I sprayed more bug-spray onto my head. We had relocated high enough on the hillside so that I could smoke, and she waved it away from her face when it blew near.

'I always wanted to trick some girl into ingesting Spanish Fly, like when I knew we'd be around each other-'

'Or, like, alone?' she asked, pinching my ears, her fingers doused in bug spray.

'Well, this was in Junior High and High School, so it would've been at a party or school function or something.'

'In the fantasy?'

'Yeah, unless it was like, you know, fantasy fantasy,' making an obscene gesture with my hand, 'in which case, yeah, alone, all alone, sure. But so have this girl-'

'Any specific girl?'

'Well, sure, certain girls for certain time periods.'

'Like what? Who? When?'

'You wouldn't know any of them.'

'It helps the story.'

'Pick a grade.'

'Sixth.'

'Kezia Daza.'

'Okay, Kezia. Go.'

'So I'd wanna trick her or like, slip her a Mickey or something, get her to ingest the Spanish Fly and then, I dunno, she'd like attack me or something.'

'Physically. Sexually. You thought she'd sexually attack you?'

'Right, yeah, something like that. And remember that Christian girls did not have libidos without …. inducement.'

'From Spanish Fly she'd, what, pin you to the ground and tear off your clothes?'

'Well, she wouldn't need to pin me, I'd of been willing, remember. But, I dunno, she'd come over to me and lead me by the hand-'

'By the crotch.'

'Sure, but lead me into a janitor's closet or secluded room in the house, if it were a house party, you know?'

'Were there other boys around?' She slapped at a bug that was too close to her eyes.

'When I'd give her the Spanish Fly?'

'Yeah,' she said, chewing on a blade of grass, her forearm slung over her forehead, looking up at the sky, the sun gone and the moon rising as big as we'd been promised.

'It depends. Not in the fantasy,' making another obscene gesture which the little girl to our right saw that time. Her mother, too, who was smoking and who covered the girl's eyes and gave me a nasty look, though I'd stopped with the gesture by then. 'But I guess in the fantasy, the party, school-mixer fantasy, yeah, there'd be other kids around.'

'Did you ever sincerely think of trying to buy Spanish Fly and actually trying to trick a girl into ingesting it?, I guess is what I'm asking.'

I pondered. 'Yeah, I'd say I had some sincerity about it. I did some internet searches and checked some encyclopedias, but all I found was that actual Spanish Fly is a myth, and the only products around like it are sold by the same people that sell like, bigger dick cream or longer erection pills or legal weed or whatever.'

'So in your head,' she continued, 'when you thought about actually buying a Spanish Fly-like product and actually getting a girl to ingest it, were there other girls and boys around, in the fantasy? In your head?'

'Sure, there would have had to have been. The Christians didn't like boys and girls getting together without an abundance of company.'

'Or your parents,' she scoffed.

'Sure.'

'So why, if there were so many boys around, did you think . . . . Kezia Daza?'

'Mm hm.'

'-would cozy over to you and demand what she needed from *you*?'

'I dunno,' I said. 'I just …. it was a fantasy.'

'Spanish Fly would make a girl horny, not make her lose her mind.'

'Ouch.'

'Sorry. Just, you know,' she said, half-heartedly patting my leg. 'I didn't mean-'

'Yeah.'

'No, I mean. Aw, that was mean of me. Shit.'

'There's been plenty of ladies who've lost their mind over that shit right there,' Manfred said, appearing from the tall grass, pointing at me with the hand that held a smoldering cigarette, wiping wine from his chin with the back of his other hand, which held a silver thermos. 'Or at least temporarily thrown caution to the wind,' he continued, 'consequences and standards be damned-'

'Lord,' I said.

'Yowza,' chimed Victoria.

'-recklessly abandoned scruples and principles,' Manfred resumed, undeterred, 'audaciously turned a blind eye to good taste-'

'What did you do, eavesdrop on us with a thesaurus?' Victoria asked, laughing.

'-brashly bid *adieu* to her romantic fantasies-'

'We were just talking about those,' she said.

'-with daring, devil-may-care, uninformed zeal,' Manfred persevered as I spied a piece of notebook paper wrapped around the thermos of wine, 'showing little or no prudence, hastily and with a steaming, heaping pile of negligence, thrown herself heedless and headlong-'

'What's on that piece of paper, Puffer?'

'-into an ill-advised, rash and altogether fruitless, madcap adventure-'

'For fuck's sake!' The woman who'd seen me making the obscene gesture was tired of it.

'-and given up the ghost and given in to the sweet, soulful love of Jonah the Caucasian, son of Amittai and Junia.'

He ground the cigarette out and I held out my open hand. He picked it up, tossed it to me, and I placed in the plastic film canister that was our temporary ashtray. He washed his mouth out with a swallow of wine, then smiled, his teeth stained purple.

'How was it?' I asked.

'The nap?'

'Yeah.'

'It's not over.'

'*In medias res?*'

'Si si, si si.'

'We're out of wine,' Victoria told him, snatching the thermos and the final swig.

'*Mea culpa, mea culpa,*' he said, parting the tall grass and disappearing as it closed behind him.

Whatever band was on stage was generic enough to not be disruptive, either by being too catchy or not so at all. The coffee I was drinking had gone cold but I did not mind. The festival's organizers had affixed a large peace sign in the tree to the left of main stage, where its branches hung over the crowd. White Christmas lights had been wrapped around the sign, affixed the wood on all sides. From where we lay it sat just below the plump moon, the moon itself just over yonder tree line.

Victoria sighed and cupped the back of her head in her hands, looking skyward. 'And you never found it.'

'Spanish Fly.'

'Mm.'

'No. I stopped looking, though. Could be out there.'

'Where?'

'I think most people just use alcohol.'

'You should trick Julie Jacklet into ingesting some.'

'Alcohol.'

'Jonah.'

'What?'

'No, I mean give her some Jonah.'

'But first alcohol.'

'Of course.'

It was dark enough that we did not see Julie until she was lying down beside us, stealing a cigarette from the pack of mine that lay in the grass.

The band that had been playing had finished their set and were breaking down while the next band waited to set up. The walkway was crowded and I deferred my porta-john venture.

The walkway was six-feet wide and just a well-trodden stretch of the hillside where grass had been stamped out by so many feet. It served as a boundary between those really interested in watching and listening to the acts on stage and those who wanted to smoke or talk. There were not any signs that instructed us where or where not to smoke, but it was understood.

'Julie Jacklet,' I said, 'how's the horse business?'

Julie did not respond when I asked her ridiculous questions, just grinned and looked away, ashing her cigarette.

'Who'd you run into?' Victoria asked her.

'Rhoda?' she responded, not sure if Victoria knew who Rhoda was.

Victoria shook her head and squinted to indicate that she did not know who Rhoda was.

'That girl milks the cow,' I said.

'Is that anything like a Newtown Creek?' Victoria jeered.

'Not even close, baby.'

'She was Manfred's girlfriend in high school. What was that?' turning to me, 'junior year?'

'Mm, I think senior,' I said. 'What's the Rhodester up to?'

The Rhodester, Julie Jacklet told us, was up to everything.

Boyfriend of one year ('Who, remind me later, Jonah,' whispering to me at an opportune moment when Victoria was overcome with a sneezing fit, 'would like Manfred to know he's not fooled-' 'The boyfriend isn't?' I asked hurriedly. 'Yeah, the boyfriend 's not fooled,' she continued, Victoria really bellowing them out now, the sneezes, 'when Manfred leaves ambiguous, automated-like messages on their machine-' 'He's still doing that? Of course!' '-especially when they're obviously not automated,' – and Rhoda worked for the phone company so she should know – 'but lamely improvised. Plus they both recognize his voice.' 'So what am I to remind you of?')

'To tell Manfred,' Julie said quickly as Victoria, having finished, was wiping her hands on the grass.

'Tell him what?' Victoria asked.

'About Rhoda and her beau,' I said. 'She's got a new beau.'

Julie sighed, relieved that my cover had worked, and stole another of my cigarettes.

Anyway, Julie went on to tell, wondering aloud if she should wait until Manfred were around so she didn't have to tell it twice, though he'd of course run into and be chatting with Rhoda anyway at some point.

'Though maybe not,' shrugging and dropping me a wink Victoria could not see, 'but anyway Rhoda's sister, Ronda, was there as well, and *she* had eloped just a year and a half ago with some pencilly little brainiac – Rhoda's words – and there were kind of living on the lam since he had some gambling debts and Ronda never paid her student loans.'

'And Rhoda Wertle,' Julie finished, 'is kind of always on the lam, you know? Remember that kid Chad?'

'Her last name is Wertle?' Victoria was amused.

'Yeah, with an E.'

Victoria laughed, triumphant, and settled back down on her back in the grass. I asked Julie Jacklet what, since we've heard what Ronda was up to, what is Rhoda, the Wertle I knew best, up to?

'You're not planning on running into and chatting with her?'

'You say she has a boyfriend?'

'Of a year,' she said, frowning. Then brightening, 'But he's not here.'

'I was just about to ask.'

'I figured you were.' Another smile.

'Ah, no, go ahead and tell me. I don't care about talking with her. I just like the looking.'

'She's still something to look at, *mon frere*.'

'*Mon frere?*'

'It means, 'My brother," Victoria said to the sky before Julie could answer, her voice sounding as though from far away.

What Rhoda was up to, Julie Jacklet said, besides the boyfriend who-

'Who what?' I asked, interrupting her before she could launch into the tale about Manfred and the answering machine while Victoria was not violently sneezing and looking where to wipe the mucus.

'Who, as I was saying, Jonah,' Julie said, grinning lightly, 'who works as a freelance photographer all over the U.S. and Europe.'

'Just like Manfred wanted to do!' I slapped Julie on the knee.

'Mm hm. And,' she continued, 'Rhoda is getting work as a booty dancer in white supremacist rap videos.'

'White supremacist rap videos?' Victoria and I echoed in unison.

'Whose ever heard of a white supremacist rap video?'

'I guess there's some label owned by this supremacist guy from Duke or something.' She yawned, the sky overhead a blanket, and stole another cigarette.

'David Duke?'

'Yeah, yeah, not Duke University but yeah, David Duke.'

'And he's signed rappers?' Victoria was curious.

'I guess.' Julie was less interested than any one else in the details of her own story.

'I would've just expected .... I dunno,' I said, bewildered at what sort of acts David Duke's record label would sign. 'Skynyrd?'

'Maybe it's all minstrel shows,' Victoria wondered aloud. 'Blackface and stuff.'

'Ugh.' Julie killed her cigarette in the soil and passed the butt to me for disposal.

'Is Rhoda a white supremacist?' Victoria plainly did not know Rhoda. Or white supremacists.

'Can't be,' I said, 'can it? I mean, I guess I haven't seen her in a few years. And I don't know this new man she's towing around.'

'Oh,' Julie said, balking, 'neither of them are white supremacists. Rhoda 's just always wanted to work as a booty dancer. She said it was you, Jonah-'

'Me?'

'Jonah?'

'Yeah, she said it was Jonah who gave her the confidence to pursue it. She said you were always ready to watch her practice and give tips.' Julie was holding her laughter, but only barely.

'Of course. An attractive girl requests to booty dance for you? It would be wicked to deny her.'

'-and so she practiced them in front of her mirror-'

'Wasn't she dating Manfred at this time?' Victoria got around to the relevant information.

'No, this was way later, when they would hang out like twice a year,' I said.

'-and watched all the booty dancing rap videos she could find-'

'And I guess it wouldn't matter if they *were* dating,' Victoria surmised. 'He did tell me I could do whatever I like with you, Jonah, whenever I wanted.'

'He's a good man.'

'-and sent out lots of audition tapes to any contest or agency or whatever there was, and David Duke's record company called her back.'

'She was unstoppably talented.' I was adamant.

'With her booty.' Victoria requested clarification.

'Yeah, and I haven't seen her perform in years. Did she ever perform for you, Julie Jacklet?'

'Ah, me and like twenty other people. Here, actually-'

'Falcon Ridge?'

'Yeah, like four, five years ago when me and Manfred would come with the Town Shop-'

'And sleep over there?' I asked, pointing to where the tents and trailers were stationed, in the far corner of the parking lot and hillside, along Route 22.

'Yeah.'

'Where did she perform for you, Jonah?' Sitting upright, Victoria searched through her bag for an errant item.

'In the parking lot of the gas station-'

'She booty danced at your gas station?' She was aghast and impressed. 'How many people were there?'

'Only me and Manfred. And some customer in the store fixing a coffee. It was like two in the morning. We were .... 18? 19?'

'And she just-'

'She asked me if I wanted to see her perform, and I did, so she hiked up her coat, bent over and ..... worked.' Julie's face was red with swelling laughter. I pointed to her shouting 'I know you love it, Julie Jacklet!' She held her mouth with the hand that was holding her cigarette, trying not to laugh and choke on the drag just inhaled.

'What was the name of that place?'

'The Sleazy.'

'The *Nice* 'n Sleazy,' Julie corrected. It had been the best job I'd had thus far, those graveyard shifts, along with the fluorescent lights and the late night people of Lafayette, NY, passing time in the convenience store on the outskirts of the empire.

*

Manfred dreamed a sordid dream; a dream he felt was not his. He dreamed of a painful place, and when asked, after several hours without even an offer of a damp cloth, Aren't you going to miss drink and detest withdrawal for however long we want to keep you here [this from stern men in serious suits and uniforms]?, he bravely responded

that getting drunk was only a way to prove that one had *done* something with one's time, one's night, one's day; and also a way of saying
that tomorrow was of no consequence at all.

He dreamed of a painful place, and that when asked, pictures of
Victoria and his mother and sisters flashing on the wall in a *macabre*
and sentimental slide-show, How do you think your family feels about
your drinking?, How does Victoria feel about your lousy drinking?,
he confidently responded that they did not want him to stop getting
drunk, they only wanted getting drunk to stop being a problem for
him.

*

Victoria did not look as though she came from the South. Her accent
more resembled a New England protestant than Southern belle, with
her articulate and intelligible dialect.

Julie Jacklet, gone to the Ladies' portable room, had been gone
longer than anticipated and I was anxious for the coffee she was re-
trieving me. The band that had been waiting to go on was on and
about to begin. The air was almost wet with black sweetness, stars
overhead animated with light.

'You mean "intelligent" I hope,' she said.

'I don't think I did.' I lay on my back, picking grass from the hillside. She had lived in Strom, Mississippi; Goldwater, Alabama; and
Wallace, Tennessee.

'And Elmodel, Georgia,' she added, snapping her fingers and wax-
ing an accent. 'And Mer Rouge, Louisiana, boy, where there ain't
enough to bother learning what the hell ain't there.'

'Down Louisiana.'

'All the way down, boy.'

The band on stage was playing what we both thought of as
schmaltz. 'Schmaltz-folk, there's another one,' she said.

'Like schmaltz-country without the amazing lap steel guitar play-ers.'

She turned on her side and asked me how I felt about the South. Like, compared with how I felt about Canada or Yemen or Australia.

'I love the South,' I said. 'Like you might love a sibling you don't see a lot or even at all. But I'm afraid of the South, too. I'm a racist, a bigot against the South. I'm ignorant about it. I see trailer parks and hopelessness.'

'Yeah, maybe 'cause you guys destroyed everything in the War of Northern Aggression.'

'....'

'I know I know you can't get behind the side that wanted slavery.'

'Or at least the side in which you could see the slavery going on in a house or a field, any old day.'

'Instead of in a coal mine or assembly line.'

Looking at Dixie, I thought, I can see how someone I'm in love with might not be in love with me.

'And you think you're so special,' she asked, 'so enlightened? Turning down jobs at Sitibank.' She rolled her eyes.

'Maybe you have the feeling, you become convinced that you should stand up for something. What is right, what is correct. Whatever it is that you hope that you'd stand in defiance of all your loved ones for. Not backing down.'

'And you became a charity case.'

'Yeah, sure. That's a consequence of my lifestyle choice. Not a desired consequences, but one I must own nevertheless. To a large extent, if it weren't for my choice to accept occasional charity from friends and family, I wouldn't be able to survive. That's a consequence of not working at Siti.'

'But you could've just worked the job at Siti for a while until-'

'Sure. Six months. A year. Two maybe. Four. Five year plan. Seven year goal. Just around this next corner. Over that hill.' A crew member on stage tripped and pushed askew a large light, glaring on the crowd. our faces light and shadow. I was practically chiaroscuro. 'Behind the bend. Around the way. That's when I'll be doing things I want to do. *Soon* I'll have the job that I want to have. I won't spend the majority of my conscious hours regretting what I am doing - and even being unaware of what I am doing. And then sure, I'll get that job I *really* want. I'll do something for work that doesn't irk me in a way that I cannot ignore. In a way I disagree with and loathe and cannot ignore.' An untended amplifier shuddered feedback. 'And ten years, fifteen, I'm good. Just around the next. After I do that thing and tell this guy what and.' I stood. 'Over the hill. Around the bend! It's right there!' I pointed to nowhere. 'I can almost see it! I can almost see it!'

*

The line was short at the porta-johns. I stepped inside, the door pinching my fingers and slamming closed, trap-like. I heard, from the toilet to my left, two voices: the female's giggle sounded very much like Rhoda's, I thought suspiciously. Looking closely, I saw two silhouettes, one Rhoda's size: very, very short. 'And with *booty,*' Juliet Jacklet added later. It was not difficult to ascertain the couple's intentions inside the porta-john. I wondered if I would prefer touching the porta-john, or any surface in the New York Canine Hedonistic Retreat - both possibilities left me undecided, and shuddering.

I finished, opened the door, emerged, spying the new issue of *Bahai'llujah* lying on the ground outside. Fine porta-john material.

*

Julie Jacklet and Puffer were still absent upon my return to the hillside, and I lay down beside Victoria to watch the sky. I used to believe that shooting stars fell all night every night, I told her, but that I had never carefully watched the stars save for summers at Camp Berea.

'Your family's camp?'

'Right.' I would lay in the softball field, I told her, after most everyone but some of my younger cousins had retired. Uncle Kaant and Aunt Heather snoring like Rototillers in their tent in the forest beyond the field. Above me the Milky Way and just dozens of careening stars and comets and meteors, just tearing the place up.

'Do you feel better for having extracted yourself from life?' She was abrupt, confrontational.

'Whoa.' I lost my breath. 'How do you mean?'

'You know how you are. You don't develop ties with people.'

'We're not tied?'

'We share close, personal moments, but we have no real commitment to each other to participate in each other's lives.'

'We're not dating.'

'Exactly,' she said, 'that's what I mean. It's not just couples that have those kinds of relationships. Only that's the way *you* see it. There's only one end-all, be-all, sacrifice-all for relationship, and all the others carry no weight. Or limited weight. I don't want to sound harsh.'

'No,' I said, 'that's right on, I guess.'

'And even with Eveline, you don't really pursue it, you just don't let it die. You find ways around communicating directly, like all those letters you guys sent back and forth when you practically lived next door. The postcard you had to hold up to a mirror to read or. Didn't she send you her birth announcement?'

'Long time back.' Victoria never allowed me to forget the five years I'd spent wooing Eveline, my first and only love - who remained unwooed and, now, was gone - save Victoria's reminders.

'But, like, *her* birth announcement, from like twenty-whatever years ago, the one her mom would've sent out about her birth, Eveline's.'

'It was a good find. I was pleased to see it.'

'It's kinda....'

'She's an archaeologist of her own history.'

'And yours and Puffer's.' I rinsed my mouth with a violent cup of coffee. It was like swallowing bad breath. She changed topics. 'What was it that happened with you and him?'

'Puffer?'

'Yeah.'

'Eh,' I shrugged, 'nothing really happened. We just, I dunno, dimmed out a while. I was getting work writing for Darko's paper-'

'How long ago was that? You never even see him anymore.'

'I saw him just the other day, actually. Still Darko.'

'You saw him in Brooklyn?'

'Yeah, I was outside the park with Marcenda-'

'You saw *Marcenda* in *Greenpoint*?' She sat up.

'Rather accidentally. This was all before the demonstration. We wouldn't have seen each other at all if I hadn't of stepped on her dog.'

'Bolivar? You stepped on Bolivar?'

'Killed him, actually.' I chuckled, remembering the pleasure I'd taken, pure and without malice, at the serendipity of the event; then felt the flood of guilt and all that other.

'This is what the hell I'm talking about, Jonah,' she said, hitting me. 'You run into a crazy ex - *whom we gave a ride out of the city on the way here* - and kill her fucking dog and you haven't brought it up yet?'

I explained to Victoria that since I had killed the very dog I had always wanted to kill, and had done so on a lovely day in Greenpoint in the presence of Marcenda, and that we were levitating fifteen feet off of the ground-

'Fuck you,' she said. 'Fuck you levitating.'

-and because of all of this, I didn't think she'd believe the tale and I wasn't going to do it disservice by not telling the whole thing, so I'd opted to just refrain, until she'd tricked me into-

'Into talking about what goes on in your life?' She stared at me dramatically.

'Did anyone see you, up there, levitating?'

'Sure, I saw Darko, like I just said. And Bea brought me a coffee.'

'Where was the dog?'

'It was on the sidewalk, being fought over by a crow and some squirrels and then a big dog.'

'So this girl had to watch her dog . . . . Why didn't you shoo them away?'

'We were levitating.'

'Why didn't you ask Bea for help?'

'She's an old woman. She works too much anyway, and shouldn't have to clean up a dog that I killed just because I was levitating.'

'Uncontrollably.'

'Okay, uncontrollably levitating. It's the same thing.'

'How?'

'Either way I wouldn't have asked Bea for help with the dead dog.'

'You're like that Hank Williams song,' she said, 'what's it called....'

We heard rustling in the tall grass, then the sound of two sticks striking together in 4/4 time. Then a toneless voice began to sing.

'Kawliga was a wooden Indian standing by the door
He fell in love with an Indian maiden
Over in the antique store.'

Victoria (as well as Julie Jacklet, who had just appeared out of nowhere again, laying in the grass beside us) joined Manfred - who parted the grass with his hands, shirtless, somehow a new thermos of wine in his waistband and two sticks in his fists - on the high part,

'Kaw - li - gaaaaaaa,'

while Manfred took the bass, plundering the depths of his range for the bottomless octave. He then returned to solo again.

'Just stood there and never let it show,'

Victoria and Julie adding some

> 'Ha-cha,
> Ha-cha,
> Ha-cha'

's and shook their opened hands around their heads like peacocks, strutting, Manfred finishing,

> 'So she could never answer yes or no.'

'That moon you ordered up, Puffer-' I said before he interrupted, jumping into the air, hurling the thermos into the forest and landing on his knees in the grass, howling,

> 'Poor old Kawliga, he never got a kiss
> Poor old Kawliga, he don't know what he missed,'

Victoria and Julie played an intricate patty-cake that kept a mesmerizing, playground rhythm, a pitter-patter backbeat,

> 'Is it any wonder that his face is red?,'

the girls giving a definitive and sassy, *Mm hmmm,*

> 'Kawliga, that poor old wooden head.'

*

'That moon I ordered up is shining satisfactorily,' Manfred said, settling down beside Victoria.

'This guy,' I said, turning to Victoria, 'has the most annoying girlfriend.'

Puffer laughed and she made a *That's very funny* face and rummaged through her bag. Julie Jacklet looked to be sleeping.

'Julie Jacklet,' I said, shaking her leg, 'you up?' She moaned and rolled over onto her stomach, her arms beneath her body. 'Where are my matches?' She wiggled her ass in response, and I saw the outline of the matchbook in her right pocket, so I searched the left first.

*

Scene: hillside.

'When did it happen?'

'Rhoda dancing?'

'Yeah.'

'You were there.'

'I most certainly wasn't.'

'Manfred-'

'I would remember,' Manfred said, thrusting out his chest, 'if an ex girlfriend of mine - or of anyone - performed a booty dance in my presence.'

Victoria was feigning sleep. Julie was tying pieces of grass into knots, over and over in some he-loves-me, he-loves-me-not game.

'It was in the parking lot at the Sleazy.'

'The *Nice* 'n Sleazy? Definitely not.'

'Yes, of course you don't remember.'

'Was that the night-'

'Yeah, you ate an entire calzone, straight through.'

'Stoned.'

'And you were stoned as well as gorged, and it was like two in the morning so of course you don't remember.'

'What was it like?'

'Infallible. You remember what the parking lot looked like at the time, nobody in the town around, the air thick with dew and the outside lights and lights at the gas pumps shining like nightlights and everything beyond their reach is dark and unseeable or at least only vaguely silhouetted, so it doesn't feel safe to not be in bed somewhere, asleep .... and there we were consciously looking at gravel, sucking on a cup of coffee, kicking at it with your toes, the gravel-'

'What kind of "Aw shucks" picture are you painting here?'

'And then Rhoda just pulling up her coat and bending over-'

'Blue jeans, yeah?'

'Of course. I don't think she'd of done it if she'd had normal slacks or sweatpants on.'

'No.'

'And just starts, like, you know, moving her hips and stuff and everything started doing what it does, you saw it-'

'But I don't remember.'

'The blue of her jeans riveting or like, shimmering or maybe wavelike, like an ocean-'

'Got it.

'And I dunno. That was it. It was intensely satisfying.'

'And after we left? You?' He made an obscene gesture.

'No.'

'*Por que no?*'

'You're alone in there, working the graveyard shift. You never knew when you'd have a customer.'

'Or a booty dancer.'

'You can usually tell when you'll have one of those.'

*

Scene: hillside.

Manfred and Julie slept lightly, more drunk than asleep.

I explained to Victoria that what usually happened with me and a girl was that I got interested in the girl, then I had to trick her into being interested in me.

'Why trick? Why not be yourself?'

'Have you met me?'

She made a face: *Come off it.*

'Because myself does not ordinarily seek out strange people, charm them, make them laugh, show intense interest in them, show interest in their friends and parents and pets and histories and devote vast amounts of time and energy to these pursuits. Myself does not usually do these things. But a female demands them – while also demanding that I be myself, mind you, as you have just done. So the female demands a paradox, demands the impossible: That I continue to be myself while also being the person who whines and dines her. That's why trick.'

'I think you're over-thinking this. It limits your understanding.'

'So I trick the female into being interested in me. Not because I *know* that I myself am even interested in her at this point in any significant way. But the only way to see if you want to become closer to a person is to actually *get* closer to that person. Only then can you know if you *want* to be closer to them. But then of course it's too late to go back and *not* be close with them, because you already *are* close with them. And by then I've found out, quite often unfortunately so, that I do *not* want to be close to this person. But the only way I could have found this out was by getting closer to them, which insinuates that we will continue to grow closer. So then I have to break hearts, which I don't care for.'

Victoria sighed like I were beyond the pale and it was not worth even telling me so.

'Either that, or I'm head and heels for the girl and she's yawning. I tend to attract women who are not attracted to me.'

*

In our two tents for the night (and blessed were Julie and I to not have the snoring Manfred near our sleeping bags), I asked Julie Jacklet about Chad, whom she had mentioned before.

'What about him?'

'You mentioned him right after you said that Ronda was on the lam, and I wondered if Chad were involved in that at all.'

'No, no. Rhoda just told me that he's just gotten out of prison.'

'Oh, I didn't know he'd gone.'

'Mmm.' She yawned a smile, eyes closed. 'Marijuana.'

'Goodnight, Julie Jacklet.'

'Goodnight, Jonah.'

I was in the midst of mounting her when she asked if I thought I shouldn't give her some alcohol first.

*

'I wouldn't use a verb like "crashed" in reference to what providentially happened to the car, Manfred. I wouldn't. "Crashed" implies that I, by accident or purposefully, steered the car into another car or building or lamp-post or something, which I most surely did not. It's more that another driver crashed into the car, into me, like I was God's own antagonist, and I'm all right, by the way, arms and legs all in working order, only this minor cut on my forehead that Victoria patched right up for me. I didn't know you had a first aid kit in the back seat there, underneath the laundry and bottles and McDonald's boxes and wrappers and the dog cage and hockey sticks and shovels and volumes H through T of the Oxford English Dictionary. Must have missed it all these times. But I'm all right, Victoria too, not even a scratch on her, and I checked her head to toe, I assure you, brother. But the truck that crashed into yours as I took perhaps a questionable but nowhere near what I would call "risky" left-hand turn at the town's stop light to get into the extremely narrow parking lot of the grocery store, the truck wasn't necessarily trashing the speed limit, but wasn't none too concerned with the specifics and rigidity of it, anyway, and, well, the front of the car is fine, engine and front seats, even the backseat, right as rain, though the back right window is cracked, somewhat, but still there, or, you know, there in the back seat. Victoria found it on the street afterwards still intact, somehow. It's the trunk area of the car – and it's a small car and so a very small trunk, as you well know – and the trunk is kinda . . . . Have you ever heard of a prolapsed sphincter? Okay, you haven't. Can I get a cigarette, by the way? Between me and Victoria and the other driver we went through my whole pack afterwards. Thanks. Light? Mm, okay, good, thanks. Well, the trunk is kinda not there anymore, meaning that the back lid there that you close over the trunk?, the trunk door?, well it doesn't close anymore – you can probably spot the car down there in the parking area near the tenters. From this hillside you could see God's own swimming pool. Just look for the totally elevated trunk door. . . . And the reason it doesn't close is that the side of the car in the back there, right behind the back door, got rather pushed inwards when the truck crashed into us and busted the shelf thing there in the back which is now sticking out of the trunk. You can probably see that, too, if you strain. Victoria, get Manfred's glasses, huh? And everything in the trunk went flying all over the road, though we did rescue most of it, but the book of CDs and the box of leis were run over by a garbage truck, which good thing the garbage truck was right there to tidy the mess, Victoria noted. But the text-books and Legos and cutlery and lobster trap – have you ever hunted lobster? No? – and the sack of marbles and the bottle caps and the shards of the window that asshole thief broke like what, ten months ago?, and the dog's bone and tape dispenser and all three typewriters are all safe and sound. And, as I said, Victoria and I? Just fine. And what's more important than that?'

17

The interior of Manfred Puffer's VW Gulf would have been devastated with the mud flying from the rear wheels into the air and spattering onto the opened trunk door, were it not devastated already with years of dirt, hair, garbage and, no small thing, seven years of Pressler Dog's snout slobber. Given, however, that it was only me in the backseat – Julie Jacklet gone back to her upstate abode; Victoria and Manfred in the front – the devastation was only mine. And, as my sister Tabitha could relate, I am devastation from the morning's first batted eye.

We were very much hoping no law enforcement officers cared – they would all notice, certainly – about the upraised trunk door. Additionally, we hoped these same law enforcers were unconcerned about a twenty-six year old male hanging out of the trunk cavity – the passenger side of the back of the car indented to the point of there really only being one seat left anyway – being sprayed with mud, his hair a maelstrom in the breeze, as he attempted to keep all the tiny car's possessions within the confines of the car.

Thus far we had only lost volumes K and M of the OED; a cassette player whose ability to function was dubious; one sleeping bag; one ice skate (*that* one almost pierced a tire and caused a harangue on the Taconic Parkway, believe you me!); various Tupperware; some socks and a shirt; and perhaps fifteen empty bottles of soda or juice. (These last were let go with more purpose and intent than any other items – foot-room being at minimum in the crumpled version of Puffer's jalopy – though I didn't fight too hard to keep the socks around either.)

'You're Mommy and Daddy better have some replacement ice skates, Sir, or it's the highway for you.' Puffer, though he had not used the skates in ten years, knew their value to lie in his possession of them; in their possible employ.

'They wouldn't encourage inebriated ice theatrics anyway, so you better be prepared for only a hug and a cookie.'

'What kind?' Puffer was particular about reparations.

We were treading in Julie Jacklet's wake, traversing the Taconic Parkway to the Turnpike, heading upstate, heading home. Those of us who had made a new home in the city did not forget our old home. Instead we compared the two, wondering which one would satisfy; which would offer the freedom the other denied; which was the fluid existence of poetry, and which the rigid confines of law.

18

Mr. Jonah Jeffries arrived to the gathering just twenty minutes before his lifelong friend, Mr. Manfred Puffer, who was forty minutes late. The gathering was taking place at the Jeffries' household in their upstate New York hometown of Marietta, population 3,000. (They were, it should be said, still new to the area, twenty-nine years of residence not exactly roots in these parts.) Jonah, recognizing each car parked in the driveway - and on the lawn, to Mr. Jeffries' unending annoyance - opened the back door, entered the house, and poured himself a coffee, saying hello to the assembled.

Manfred, upon arrival, found a parking spot beneath the pine trees that separated the front lawn from the back. Sticky sap from the pines dripped onto and, due to the still open trunk door, into the Gulf. Mr. Jeffries, sandwich in one hand and punch in the other, exclaimed great wonder and almost reverent ridicule for the ability of the car to remain mobile.

'Did your invitation's start time detail a time forty-minutes later than everyone else's, Puffer?' Tabitha asked as she opened the door to allow Manfred access to the house.

'Didn't know it was possible for a party to start late,' he shrugged, looking for the beverages.

'There's nothing to wet your whistle but punch, coffee or water, Puffer.' Tabitha was somewhat clairvoyant; or at least sensitive to the obvious. 'And a good party begins and ends with each guest's presence and departure.'

'Tabby, I don't know what you mean, but don't call me Puffer.'

From the living room in the front of the house Manfred heard the jovial laughter of Leora and Derik, Derik holding forth on the personal responsibilities of Afghani and Iraqi peasants, and wondered what about this party was so unique that the happy couple had traveled from Brooklyn to Syracuse to attend.

'And Jesus cried the bloated tears of the Virgin, Victoria. Awp.' Derik - or at least Leora in his stead - had made frequent trips to the punch bowl. 'I don't care if he wants you to Milk the Cow while performing a Newtown Creek. He's your man: Either own up to your obligations, or retire from the enterprise.' Derik was no slouch on the topic of romantic and marital obligations; nor at the voicing of his carefully acquired opinion.

Hearing Victoria's name, Manfred experienced the afternoon's first brilliant flash of anticipation, wondering what Victoria was doing at the Jeffries when he knew full well she had taken the train from Syracuse to New York the night before. What was in the air?

'Puffer,' Mr. Jeffries began, balancing a plate of dip and crackers in his open palm, chewing, 'would you like me to perform an exorcism on that beauty of yours in the yard?' Both men, joined by Jonah, gazed out the dining room window to the Gulf, stoic and resolute on the green summer grass.

'Does that include the filter, the oil, the brake pads, the side panel, the trunk door and labor?'

'Sure, but it does not guarantee timeliness, nor effectiveness.'

'So what am I paying for?'

'Why, the touch of a man of God, to be sure.'

Puffer sighed. 'I've got Jonah. He's at least a boy of God.'

'He's a boy, that's for sure.'

Jonah spoke up for himself. 'But the word of Lord came to Jonah, son of Amittai.'

Derik, overhearing, hollered from the next room something about Jonah mistaking the word of the Lord for the turd of the word - which were different things. Derik, though in the parsonage of the Marietta Congregational Church, inhabited for over two-decades by Mr. and Mrs. Jeffries, did not stifle his use of Christ's name in, what some might call, vain.

'Christ high on mothballs, Jonah, the word of the Lord wouldn't come to you – awp – if you were the last living prophet taking notes on Zion.' Derik swayed and held his belly, eyes momentarily closed. Belching, he stumbled back towards the living room: too much punch.

Mrs. Jeffries and Tabitha, aprons fastened round their waists, were preparing foods and drinks in the kitchen, which smelled of sweet breads and freshly cut fruit. Jonah, Manfred and Victoria had no idea of the harm that had befallen Tabitha since they had seen her last. And, being the most self-reliant bitch in all of Onondaga County, Tabitha had no need to bring it up.

Circling the dining room table, Jonah chatted with his sister Joelle and her husband Xabier about the only missing Jeffries sibling, GK, who was still running around Army bases trying to use his father's religious credentials to escape service for which he had signed up and, most damning, been paid for.

'Why doesn't he kill one bird with two stones and get an honorable discharge *and* finish his college on the new G.I. Bill?' Joelle wondered.

'You mean two birds with one stone, dear?' Xabier asked.

'Whatever Xabier,' Manfred chimed in, 'she can kill as few birds with as many stones as she likes. Don't take any guff off him, Joelle.'

Joelle assured Manfred that she took guff from *only* her betrothed; Manfred confused 'betrothed' with 'disrobed,' and the rest of the conversation went to pot.

Leaving Manfred and Mr. Jeffries to discuss the degradation and eventual (however illusory) repair of the VW, Jonah ventured into the living room, where he saw his nemesis, Karl, sitting on the loveseat, reading a Chuck Palahniuk novel. Jonah, customarily, flew into hysterics we are all quite familiar with. *Who* invited *Karl* to *my* hometown?, he asked, spittle flying from his mouth. *Who* thought it was be *fine* to have *Karl* show his face anywhere *near* the parsonage?

Leora and Victoria, who were close by but had been ignoring Karl since his arrival shortly before Jonah, thought that Karl was more embarrassed by Jonah's Karl Eats It t-shirt than his ravings, however uncomplimentary.

'And *whoo-ooooooo* thought it would be a *good* idea to seat *Karl* on *my* grandmother's loveseat instead of in the *dirt* outside with the *dogs?*' Jonah was getting carried away.

'Use your head, Jonah,' Tabitha called from the kitchen, 'we don't even have dogs. Let alone a good pile of dirt.'

'Actually,' Mr. Jeffries corrected, buttering thickly a slice of cinnamon bread, 'we have both. And as I've just discarded some wonderfully sharp chicken bones into the compost pile, I'm certain any of Jonah's friends would feel at home with the dogs sure to be rooting through the compost – and choke on the bones, you dogs!' he howled out the window in the direction of the compost, 'or sitting on any pile of dirt very close by.'

'The point, *Dad,*' Jonah rebutted, 'is *not* that Karl should be shown the hospitality of your I'm sure exquisite composting locale. I misspoke.' He cleared his throat. All present waited. 'The point is that *Karl Eats It.* Doesn't anybody in this Jeffries clan understand this? That *Karl* doesn't deserve an ant heap in Elbridge or a trash barrel in Utica, let alone the pastor's compost in Marietta?' Most of this was lost on those not from the upstate region, including Karl, who only sat on the loveseat staring at the various speakers and, occasionally, uttering 'Totally totally' in agreement with some particular sentiment.

'I *thought,*' Jonah continued, 'that we had settled this heinous error at my *first* intervention, but now here it is my *second* intervent-'

'Jonah, hold up, kid,' Tabitha interrupted, 'but this party isn't for you, so don't let it go to your head.'

'Not for me? But Mom is somehow magically discharged from Hospice care and Derik and Leora come up from Brooklyn and you make the mistake of inviting *Karl, and* there's no *booze* and you're still telling me this isn't an intervention? Tabby, come now. Fool me once. . . .'

'Won't get fooled again, right, Jonah?' Derik was ever ready with the presidential quotation.

'This gathering, Jonah-'

'Well it must be an intervention of some kind, Tabby, 'cause we're all here and I don't see any booze and-'

'You're right, Jonah. Absolutely. This gathering – this intervention – is-'

'Why are you always intervening, Tabby? You're like the CIA or something.'

'Yeah, I am, Jonah, and if I have to rendition you to the compost pile to get your mouth shut-'

'What am I, Majid Khan?'

'-so that we can carry forward Manfred's intervention-'

'*Manfred's* intervention?'

'*My* intervention?' Manfred howled.

'-then I'll Jose Padilla your ass right now!'

'Tabby!' Mrs. Jeffries was aghast. 'Punishment by compost may be one thing, but I did not raise any children who slammed others into walls, or placed them in stress positions, or made them dirty their pants just because they could.'

'And besides, Tabby, this can't be for Manfred.'

'Can't be!' Manfred was certain. 'Where's my mother? My sisters? I haven't even been drunk yet today. *And I don't even see any chairs light enough that I could pick up and throw!* What kind of a goddamned intervention is this? *Where are the chairs?*'

It was true that the Jeffries had removed all throwable chairs from the house before the intervention had begun. They knew enough about Manfred to take his most drastic threats seriously; the rest would float away like jetsam.

'And Jesus ate the thirty-pound steak, Puffer. You don't need to throw no chairs to be told you're addicted to fuckin. . . . What was it, baby?'

Leora laughed like flutes wouldn't sing. 'Alcohol, baby.'

'Right, you're fuckin addicted to alcohol, and should stop.'

'Stop? What am I, Majid Khan?'

'Manfred,' Tabitha was direct but delicate, 'this intervention was created for you, to instill in you the obvious and simple fact that alcohol has taken over your life and we all know how happy you would be without it.'

Puffer, not exactly perturbed but feeling reactionary, hurled the closest object at hand, which happened to be Mr. Jeffries' ham on white with provolone, lettuce and mustard, across the room; the meat and bread and vegetable and condiment making connection with the wall in various manners and states of cohesion. The mustard being the most disparate.

'I yell and scream and call to the son of Amittai to resolve this injustice and call my sisters, parents and closest friends over to the house with dexterity!' Puffer was articulate.

'Well, of course I have all your sisters' numbers,' Jonah stammered, 'and your mother's, but who else you mean? Julie Jacklet? Marcenda?'

'We have the house until seven, Manfred.' Tabitha resumed control. 'So keep the driving distance in mind.' No one needed any reminders on how far away from what was already the wilderness of Route 20 the drive to Marietta was.

'Awp, Jesus-'

'Baby, be soft,' Leora urged, her hands in the holes of Derik's jeans, 'he's an alcoholic, and there's not even any *booze* at this shindig!' She said 'booze' as though hitting a high note in the ecstasy of girls jumping rope in the sun.

'-you're fuckin, awp, addicted to alcohol-'

'And to Greenpoint, too.' Tabitha gave Jonah a look so direct and full of intent even Pressler Dog, who was only lying on the floor waiting to be let outside to urinate, understood its meaning.

'Yeah, Greenpoint, too, Puffer and-'

'Don't call me Puffer.'

Mrs. Jeffries, with a broad sweeping gesture of her arms - full of a large glass pan, itself full of the most satisfying macaroni and cheese this side of the *Liber de Coquina* - entered the dining room. Or that is what the Jeffries children believed, about the mac and cheese. Commenting that it was time for a snack, she placed the pan onto the table - already a byzantine of cheeses, breads, fruits, vegetables, noodles, brownies, cookies, cakes - and resumed her patrol in the kitchen of what else people would eat; though not before reminding Manfred that the only thing a boozer can attract is trouble and loose women - no offense, Victoria.

'And *whooooo-ooooo*,' Puffer was suddenly irate, 'invited *Karl* to *my* intervention? In case anyone hadn't *noticed*, I have made quite a hobby of enjoying Jonah's Karl Eats It campaigns. *Plus* it doesn't exactly *help* that all he wants to *do* is bag Victoria, who is not exactly Mother Theresa - no offense, Vic.'

Victoria told Manfred that he was not exactly condemned to die, either. Or venereally envious. And that she'd rather perform a thousand Newtown Creeks than so much as sleep in the same county as Karl.

'What am I, Majid Khan?' Karl quipped.

'Yeah,' added Tabitha, 'what is this, the Salt Pit?'

19

Walked into Manhattan, around the town. Found a street fair downtown on Broadway. Lots of food vendors, paintings, jewelry, bags, clothes. I bought a mango/banana beverage. Delicious. I was hoping to find a nice postcardish thing to send to South America but postcard vendors hadn't a spot to spit on Broadway. Wandered west and north and finally to a theater and saw Woody Allen's new movie. Which was okay and going to the movies makes me feel nice for a while, all those images and the darkness and the other-worldliness. I remember you mentioning you hadn't been to the movies in a while, and I thought at the time and still do that I wanted to take you to the movies. Then I walked uptown and looked at all the summer Sunday New York people busy on avenues, the last of the weekend, the beginning of night. Wandered to the train and then wandered on home. People grilling in the park, riding bicycles. Bars spilling with people holding drinks.

20

Dog: Otis Fritz

Breed: Basset Hound. Black/Grey/Brown

Client: Giorgi Mikolka

In Date: 07/01/06. *Out Date*: 07/11/06. 6:00pm.

Special Instructions: This dog is a smart ass, I don't care what anyone says. But I DO care that fucking Derik AND Jimmy suggested Tejas for lunch. I BELIEVE THAT I MADE IT CLEAR THAT NO ONE WAS EVER TO SUGGEST TEJAS TO COLIN EVER AGAIN! If this belly weren't so f'ing full of meat and fry I'd find my original proclamation and can all your sorry asses. What would you do without the Retreat then, huh Brittany? Huh, Hayseed? Starve, that's what. Otis' owner says don't let him play for long stretches or he becomes a power hungry asshole and attacks. This means don't mix this dog ever at all. And if Otis attacks anyone he's getting the Tejas treatment - nice going down, poison on the way out.

Colin sighed, leaning back, eyes to the ceiling but seeing nothing. The enormous desk was cluttered like hell is crowded. He was imagining his stomach as a large jungle in Vietnam sprayed with Agent Orange. An empty can of orange soda in the gray garbage bin beside him. The New York Canine Hedonistic Retreat was not busy for an early Saturday afternoon, which made Colin less task-oriented than customarily. He was so lethargic that even Derik was putting forth extra effort - meaning *some* effort - so that the Retreat did not entirely shit the bed - something Otis the Basset Hound managed to do every evening at the Retreat.

Dog: Pressler Dog Puffer.
Breed: Choluskee. Brindle.
Client: Manfred Puffer.
In Date: 07/01/06. *Out Date*: 07/13/06. 9:00pm.
Special Instructions: Pressler Dog is a very good dog. Give him treats and love - but not more than Brando!On second thought, give Pressler Dog no treats or love and all affection towards Brando! Manfred said he might leave P.Dog til tomorrow morning, though Jonah is working the overnight shift so may take P.Dog home in the morning. Jonah, do yourself a favor and check out the new dog beds that came in today. Derik and I made a lovely bed for you out of three of these new beds and packing tape. You'll sleep like you're at home - except with hundred of dogs pissing barking screaming shitting all around you! [This note from Derik, ladies: Enjoy the overnight, Jonah! Glad you could make it back to the city just in time for the 4th of July double-booked extravaganza at the NYCHR! Good luck finding tip money, hoser. Tejas was expensive! Don't be afraid of no overnight Retreat ghosts, wittle Jonah! I hear sometimes these dogs can be 'a spreachin s'anglas landadge or sprakin sea Djoytsch! Derik out,whores!]

Colin moaned.

'Shut up about Tejas!' Derik, short-winded from running up the stairs, was impatient. 'We need to know what to feed Countess Ivanovna.'

'Blug blug blug, pllllllll.' Colin was not direct.

'No making up noises! Answer! Now!'

Colin's lips vibrated spittle upwards, airborne, which then settled onto his stomach, the keyboard and monitor. 'Hummmmmmm fffff. Globp. Klliiiiink.'

'Colin! Marcenda wants to feed the Princess and if I don't tell her what brand Princess eats that woman is gonna pester me all afternoon in *hable es-pan-yoll*' - when bilingual he rolled his eyes and flicked his wrist in circles as though lassoing the language in his indifference. 'Colin! CVA! Wellness? Colin VanAndervson I'm a gonna-!' He held up his first, comically dangerous. 'Iams? Nutro? Nothing? Something! Answer!'

Colin pushed off the floor with his enormous feet, the wheeled chair rolling back to the wall, where he slam-dunked the nearest dunkable object - an unopened can of fancy wet food - and stood. 'Brando!' he shouted, his voice echoing deeply from all walls beneath the roar of the air conditioners. Brando appeared from the stairs and ran to Colin, jumping and whining in urgent affection.

'Colin, you haven't finished turnover notes. The Retreat is about to make the Greenpoint explosions look like a goddamned tea party. You cannot leave now!' Derik was assertive; and uncharacteristically concerned. 'Brittany is on shift tonight and if one more dog ends up hospitalized on her shift I think she might quit.' Colin frowned and sat.

The only place to go had been back to New York. Stay in America - the America of New York. So that is where they had come back to. Marcenda, Manfred, Jonah, Victoria. Where else in the world could one hope to hide in the open? Back they had come, Manfred and Jonah and Victoria limping across the Kosciuszko Bridge in Puffer's undead VW. Jonah had immediately called Colin and asked for help making money. Then he had called Julie Jacklet, just to stay in touch - no answer. Then Marcenda - who did answer in a torrential monologue lasting into the next day and interrupted only by lovemaking and bathroom breaks, and eventually by Jonah's having to arrive on shift at the NYCHR at 11:00pm, copies of *Handout* and *Bahai'llujah* and the latest United For Bitch and Justice newsletter under his arm. Marcenda, loquacious but willing, with nowhere to go (back to Ecuador?), stayed. As they lay on the dog beds on the floor, Jonah read her articles she was not interested in but nevertheless turned her crank (the reading aloud) before they made love on dog beds, amidst the amorous and distasteful odors and noises of caged pups.

'Sure,' Jonah read from *Handout* an article about June's demonstration on Broadway, holding a plastic cup of coffee in one hand, Marcenda's thigh in the other, 'money will use reason if that will work. Money will use violence if that will work. Money will use sweetness if that will work. Money will use sentiment or fear or politeness if they will work. Money will use money if it will work.' Marcenda, not listening, plucked the magazine from Jonah's hand and tossed it into the recycling bin, atop candy wrappers and coffee cups, dog magazines and print outs. She sat on his lap and they were lips and arms. Shifting locales, Jonah retrieved the magazine from the bin and set it aside before mounting his good lady on the floor of the Retreat - or on the beds on the floor, to be precise. Downstairs Hercules jumped in place, thick head indifferently striking the run's ceiling.

On 25th Street inebriated pedestrians staggered in ones and twos. Marcenda slept. Jonah stood on the sidewalk, listening to the city in the night hours, the minus time. Sirens uptown; clanging metal nearby; a few birds nested somewhere, hungry. Jonah waited, standing, for the sun to peek above the building's tops and shine, however thinly, on 25th Street; on his unshaven face. He rubbed his eyes and wondered where he would take Marcenda today. There were only so many places to go, even in New York; only so many things to do. Eating, laughing, walking, watching, moving, listening. People, cabs, towers, beggars, faces, feet, asses, street. Keep moving, he thought. Do something. Now, not later. Don't let it get away, wherever you've pinched it.

end